DOCTOR WHO

The Dalek Generation

P9-DDV-043

Valparaiso Public Library
103 Jefferson Street
Valparaiso, IN 46383

Also available from Broadway:

Plague of the Cybermen *by Justin Richards*

Shroud of Sorrow *by Tommy Donbavand*

BBC

DOCTOR WHO

The Dalek Generation

NICHOLAS BRIGGS

PORTER COUNTY PUBLIC LIBRARY

Valparaiso Public Library
103 Jefferson Street
Valparaiso, IN 46383

SF   BRI   VAL
Briggs, Nicholas.
The Dalek generation /
33410012383990

05/15/13

Broadway Paperbacks
New York

BROADWAY

This is a work of fiction. Names, characters, places, and incidents
either are the product of the author's imagination or are used fictitiously.
Any resemblance to actual persons, living or dead, events, or locales
is entirely coincidental.

Copyright © 2013 by Nicholas Briggs

All rights reserved.
Published in the United States by Broadway Paperbacks,
an imprint of the Crown Publishing Group,
a division of Random House, Inc., New York.
www.crownpublishing.com

Broadway Paperbacks and its logo, a letter B bisected on the diagonal,
are trademarks of Random House, Inc.

This edition published by arrangement with BBC Books, an imprint of
Ebury Publishing, a division of the Random House Group Limited, London.

Doctor Who is a BBC Wales production for BBC One.
Executive producers: Steven Moffat and Caroline Skinner.

BBC, DOCTOR WHO, and TARDIS (word marks, logos, and devices) are
trademarks of the British Broadcasting Corporation and are used under license.
Cybermen originally created by Kit Pedler and Gerry Davis.

Library of Congress Cataloging-in-Publication Data is available upon request.

ISBN 978-0-385-34674-0
eISBN 978-0-385-34675-7

Printed in the United States of America

Editorial director: Albert DePetrillo
Series consultant: Justin Richards
Project editor: Steve Tribe
Cover design: Lee Binding © Woodlands Books Ltd. 2013
Production: Alex Goddard

1   3   5   7   9   10   8   6   4   2

First Edition

For Steph and Ben,
my two favourite human beings

Prologue
Crash on Sunlight 349

It was another beautiful, sunny day on the planet Sunlight 349, as Lillian Belle set off on her latest assignment.

If she was honest with herself, the fact that *every* day on Sunlight 349 was 'another beautiful, sunny day' was perhaps a little tedious. Mind you, whenever she had such thoughts, she would force herself to remember what life had been like for her parents. They had lived on the edge of starvation for the first thirty years of their lives. In squalor. On a freezing cold, polluted planet whose name no one even wanted to remember.

When Maizie and Alfred Belle had been given the chance to move to Sunlight 349, for them, it had truly felt like dying and going to heaven. Lillian knew this because, although she had been only seven months old at the time, her parents had, over the years, often told her how they had felt... And there had been tears in their eyes as they remembered.

Maizie and Alfred had died just about four years

ago now, within months of each other. They had been a devoted couple, proud to see their only daughter become a journalist. Moving to Sunlight 349 had brought them such incredible happiness. Every morning, they would stand on their tiny balcony and look out over the calm, ordered, pastel-shaded symmetry of the vast city in which they lived, and give thanks for the Dalek Foundation and the Sunlight Worlds.

The Dalek Foundation had given them another chance, another life. And although the ill effects of the squalid conditions their bodies had previously been forced to endure had ultimately meant that their lifespans were relatively short, they had both died contentedly in their early 60s.

So Lillian felt guilty when she found the pastel shades... dull. Cross with herself, when she longed for the temperature to vary by a few degrees now and again.

Sometimes she almost prayed for rain. She had never experienced it. She had seen it on screens, read about it in books. She had even stood in her shower, dialled down from hot to cold, closed her eyes and tried to imagine what it might be like if this were the weather outside – all day!

The skimmer-bus, touching down gently, jolted Lillian out of her daydream. The railroad official sitting opposite gave her a strange look. Lillian could not resist a smirk to herself. She realised she had been sitting with her face up, eyes closed and twitching at the imaginary impacts of those longed-for raindrops.

'Something the matter?' asked the official.

'No,' she said, still smirking a bit.

Then she felt guilty again. She glanced around at the grim faces of other officials on the bus and remembered there was a serious business in hand. She tried to suppress the fact that because it *was* serious, and perhaps even a little dangerous, she wanted to jump for joy. Everything was so smooth-running and happy on Sunlight 349; and that made a journalist's job pretty uninteresting.

At last, there was the potential for bad news...

As she stepped out of the bus, she was only dimly aware of the door whirring shut and the soft hiss of the vehicle lifting off and flying away behind her. The concerned mutters of the crowd were also fading for Lillian.

She was transfixed by the disaster site before her.

Two trains had collided. At speed. The impact had torn into both vehicles, ripping them apart in the front sections, then scattering the rear carriages into each other; hammering, crushing, tearing them out of shape. Only the very last compartment of the left-hand train still retained any semblance of its original outline. The rest was just wreckage. A horrible snapshot of metal, plastic and fibres, twisted, bent and pulverised by unrelenting kinetic force.

People had died in this crash, Lillian knew there was no doubt about that. Then she realised, with some shame, that a number of the supposed 'officials' she had travelled with were in fact relatives of the survivors or victims. And she had allowed herself a warm grin of satisfaction at the exciting professional prospects such a disaster offered her. For a moment, her own selfishness made her feel sick. But the exhilaration was still there, and she pressed on, seeking out security guards to get permission to inspect the wreckage.

She already had her tiny palm-holo-camera running. She panned across the entangled trains and pulled back for a wide shot of those looking on, many of them featureless with shock, some starting to cry, gulping in painful air in great heaving sobs. The sound of their grief flooded into her ear implants – perfect, stereo human suffering. She zoomed in on one old lady, for an instant thinking it was her mother. It could so easily have been, a few years back. It made her feel lucky… and guilty yet again. That old guilt about not feeling grateful enough for the Sunlight Worlds.

A security guard touched her on her elbow. It made her jump a little.

'This way,' he nodded, and led her down the slope to the track.

As she followed him, she saw emergency crews arriving and going about the morbid business of removing bodies. There was the smell of fire, scorched metal and worse. Electronic cutting gear was starting up; slicing into metal so that any survivors could be rescued. She heard cries of pain, of alarm, of relief. More emergency crews arrived, skimmer lights flashing, sirens wailing and then cutting off suddenly, as if in shock, as the vehicles descended gently beside the broken, twisted tracks.

She was still filming, drifting sideways, not sure if it was the gentle incline leading to the crash site or her own insatiable curiosity that was pushing her on. She almost collided with a man in emergency service uniform. He was of some kind of supervisory rank, it seemed, from the insignia on his black, plastic-sheened uniform.

'That's far enough,' he said, his voice muffled behind his helmet visor.

'Lillian Belle, *Sunlight 349 Holo-News*,' she said, still filming.

'I know,' he replied, somewhat emotionlessly. 'Daniel Ash, site supervisor. You don't want to go any further. Trust me.'

'Will you talk on camera?' she asked, focusing on him, the auto-systems of her camera struggling to fix on his visor or his obscured face behind it.

'Sure. There's been a train crash. Not much more to say. We don't know how many are dead. We're finding survivors. A lot of injured. All local hospitals are on full alert. Emergency protocols are working well. How am I doing?'

'Any word on the cause of the crash?' she asked, panning right onto the closest piece of wreckage. A survivor, in terrible pain, was being helped out through a half-collapsed window. She quickly defocused and returned to Daniel Ash's troublesome visor. He was looking at her blankly.

'What do you want me to say?' he asked. 'Two trains crashed. One of them shouldn't have been on this track, I guess. We're just worrying about who's left alive so far.'

At that moment, Lillian felt the heat and vibration

of something powerful whooshing overhead. She instinctively tilted her camera view upwards into the sky, and caught the shimmering blue of the underside of an airborne Dalek as it flew over the crashed trains.

She and Daniel Ash simply paused for a moment, watching the Dalek come to a halt, as it suspended itself in mid-air. Then it descended; its bronze, metallic, conical armour glimmering in the constant sun as its mid-section and head-dome rotated. Scanning, watching, assessing...

Everyone on the Sunlight planets was familiar with the Daleks. They were not seen very often, but everyone knew them as the representatives of the great and good Dalek Foundation. The saviours of a generation that had been scarred and displaced by galactic economic and political collapse. There was always admiration for the idea of the Daleks, Lillian had grown up with that, but actually seeing them, encountering them, was always an oddly unsettling experience. No one was in any doubt that they were a force for good. No one.

But...

Squat, undeniably brutal in their outward appearance, these ambassadors of charity and philanthropy always seemed to tease at a sense of dichotomy in human minds. That these creatures who looked so ready for conflict should be the purveyors of such kindness and optimism seemed such a self-evident mismatch. And yet, it was true. The Daleks had saved and enhanced countless billions of lives.

'Report!'

Lillian and Daniel heard the signature sound of the

Dalek's voice echo across the wreckage; its staccato, electronic tone seeming peculiarly at home amongst the torn and shredded train remnants.

'I *thought* we might see them here,' said Daniel, nodding.

'Because this never happens?' asked Lillian, pointedly.

'Yes.' And Daniel started to draw away, signalling to a subordinate nearby to take over supervising Lillian.

'Any news on the drivers?' Lillian pressed further, halting Daniel's retreat. He paused for a moment, perhaps considering if it was wise to divulge something, she thought. And then she was sure. Yes, he was deciding whether or not to tell her something important. He clocked the look on her face and she fancied that he looked a little caught out.

'They...' he hesitated for an instant. 'They both ejected. They're safe. In shock, but...' He trailed off as he hurried away, calling out to some medics tending to an injured passenger. Lillian filmed him as he was engulfed by the milling masses of emergency workers, wounded, dead and dying. She carried on, unflinching, even as Daniel's subordinate put a firm, gloved hand on her shoulder.

'OK, that's it,' she heard his muffled voice say, through another visor. She instantly turned to speak to him, but he clearly knew what was coming. 'No,' he said, firmly. 'You go back up to the top.'

'Will the Dalek be coming over here?' Lillian asked. They both glanced round. It had now disappeared, over the other side of the wreckage.

Daniel's subordinate gave her a 'you must be joking' look. 'When was the last time you saw a Dalek give an interview?' he asked, evidently not expecting an answer, as he pushed her up the incline, towards the rest of the onlookers.

It was a fair point, she thought. She had never seen a Dalek interviewed for holo-television.

As she reached the top of the incline, constantly recording the blank, drained faces of the onlookers, she heard, just for a moment, incoherent, muffled, grating echoes from the other side of the crash site. The Dalek was talking, but Lillian doubted she would ever find out what it was saying or to whom it was speaking.

On the other side of the wreckage, well shielded from the sights and sounds of the rescue operations, the Dalek waited, motionless. A security guard walked up to it, obediently, presenting it with a small, black sphere.

'The journey recorder,' said the guard, a little nervously.

Before the guard could hand the sphere over, some force from within the suction cup at the end of the longest of the Dalek's metallic protuberances came into play. It sucked the sphere into contact with the cup. There was a faint, electronic, tingling vibration. Not so much a sound as a tangible needling of the air. The guard winced a little. The vibration stopped.

The bronze dome at the top of the Dalek swivelled slightly, its mechanisms purring with cool precision. The eyestalk twitched. The blue iris on the outward-facing edge of the black ball of the lens attachment seemed to squint with a narrowing disdain.

'Where is the driver of this train?' demanded the Dalek. 'You said you would bring him to me.'

'He's on his way. He's... he's in... in shock,' the guard found himself stammering to explain. There was something about the Dalek that made him feel he was under suspicion. 'He's had a terrible... Er, the medics are...'

'Where is he?' the Dalek demanded again, a fierce note of anger invading its electronic articulation.

The guard couldn't think of anything else to say. He merely stared at the Dalek, ideas for words choking in his throat; veins beginning to stand out around his increasingly watering eyes.

The silence was broken by the sphere suddenly detaching from the Dalek's sucker cup. It thudded onto the hard, baked soil, discarded. The guard started to kneel to pick it up.

'Leave it there!' commanded the Dalek, now swivelling its dome violently; tilting its eyestalk up and down impatiently.

Two medics arrived, gently ushering a shocked-looking young man forward.

'I'm afraid Mr Sezman is suffering from shock,' explained one of the medics.

The Dalek repositioned its eyestalk, focusing on the medic. It edged forwards a little, emitting a truncated metallic whine as it did so. The medic nearly stumbled backwards at this, but stood his ground.

'He has to go to hospital immediately,' he explained further.

The Dalek paused for a few moments, surveying the small group of four humans. Mr Sezman, the driver, swayed a little. One of his knees appeared to buckle under his own weight. The medics quickly strengthened their grip on his arms to support him.

But before they could fully straighten Mr Sezman up, a harsh burst of energy emitted from the shortest of the Dalek's metal attachments. Funnelling towards them in a focused beam, the discharge burst around them all, burning bright, crackling and spitting like a shower of ice on white hot metal. All four of them contorted in terrible, silent agony for an instant, their jagged forms flickering painfully, caught in a photo-negative image, blue-tinged and merciless; so bright their skeletons bleached through it. Then the harsh light and sound faded fast as their lifeless bodies fell to the ground.

Unconcerned, the Dalek immediately took off; a directly vertical course at high speed, leaving its victims to be found amongst the wreckage. Unexplained deaths, to be referred to the Dalek authorities for investigation...

An investigation that would never happen.

Chapter One
Death on Gethria

Whirling through the Vortex, dwarfed by the infinities of eternity and a limitless universe, a small, blue, cuboid object, with a glowing light atop and windows like white, squarish eyes squinting out into a dizzying, kaleidoscopic tunnel, propelled itself ever onwards.

It was the TARDIS, space-time craft of that most mysterious citizen of the universe, the Doctor. Inside that sturdy, blue exterior, exactly engineered to resemble a twentieth-century London police box's modest dimensions, there was an Aladdin's Cave of impossibly advanced technology and seemingly endless accommodation.

At its heart was the control room. Here, on top of a glass-floored platform sat the TARDIS's multi-sided console. Dancing around it with a fevered intensity, punctuated by spectacularly carefree flourishes and pirouettes, was the Doctor himself. Making adjustments, tweaking an intricate imbalance here, absently flicking a switch or two there, he always took great pride in operating his beloved time and space machine. They had been together for many lifetimes. Many Earthly companions had come and gone, but the Doctor and the TARDIS... they were constants in each other's lives.

His life's work had been the accidental but well-meaning interference in the lives of others. He had illegally set off into the universe, defying the laws of his now extinct people, the Time Lords, because he wanted to *explore*... to seek out... anything and everything.

He had experienced the extremes of existence. There had been so much terror, so much delight... and everything in between.

He had made so many friends, fought as many enemies. There had been beginnings and ends, joyous meetings, sad farewells. And it was all etched across the face of this man who had had many faces. The one, unchanging facet of his appearance – the scope of his lives and deeds, there in his eyes. There, in the warmth of his ancient smile.

Even now, with the Doctor in his most outwardly youthful body, more than ever, there was something of the ancient about him. There was a weariness... Perhaps even a growing awareness of his place in all things, that made him concerned about the extent of the consequences of his wanderings.

Travelling alone now, he was intending to keep a low profile in the tracks of eternity. Those were his avowed, good intentions.

But the Doctor's Achilles heel was his curiosity.

Standing back from the console, exuding that pride in his own, latest adjustments, he caught sight of himself in the glass column ascending from the centre of the hexagonal console. The unmistakable signs of his ship's power were rising and falling encouragingly inside the glass. He beamed a broad smile at himself, tweaked his bow tie and smoothed down his tweed jacket.

'Somewhere nice and quiet, I think,' he said to his reflection. He twiddled his fingers, like a safe-cracker about to unlock a fortune. But before he could set a new course, something on one of the festooned hexagon's opposite surfaces bleeped.

A single, faint bleep. Then another. And another, until the bleeping became insistent, bordering on the downright irritating.

The Doctor had already circled the console and was anxiously inspecting the source of the bleeping. A blinking amber light. He frowned and tapped it. The bleeping and blinking continued.

'Are you sure, old girl?' he whispered, moving his ancient, youthful face closer and closer to the amber light. This was not a light he had ever thought to see blinking again. Then, suddenly, it stopped. No blinking. No bleeping.

'Oh,' said the Doctor. He felt a sudden pang of sadness; but it was only momentary, because the silence was soon broken by a very distinct tapping on the outer side of the TARDIS's wooden doors. Something was outside, in the surging Vortex, tapping on the TARDIS's outer dimensions.

Checking that the ship's force field was in place, the Doctor dashed from the console, down the steps to the rather quaint wooden doors set into the other-worldly architecture of the control room. He flung the doors open, and there, hovering before him was a small white, glowing cube.

'Oh, you're just a baby one, aren't you?' he said, beaming with his unique mix of surprise, delight and enthusiasm. In an instant, he had snatched the cube into his hands, thrown the doors shut and dashed back up the stairs to the controls. He held the cube in the light from the console, squinting, intrigued.

In dire emergencies, his people had used these strange, telepathic cubes to send messages. He had used one himself, many lifetimes ago – and not so long ago, he had been lured into a trap by one. But this little 'fellow' was a slightly different kettle of fish, he thought.

It was very small. About half the size of your standard Time Lord cube.

'Looks like something I might have knocked up in a hurry,' he said to himself. 'Ah!'

And the thought hit him.

Or rather… the question. Was this one of those moments when something from his future had rocketed back into his past?

Time travel was fraught with these difficulties. He had no way of telling when and where the cube had come from just by looking at it. Best to press ahead and find out what this little messenger had to say to him, he thought.

Crouching down on the floor, with all the inelegance of a recently born gazelle, the Doctor placed the cube in front of him and began to concentrate his whole mind upon it. Would it work, he wondered? If it did, it would be a sure sign that he had indeed sent the message to himself.

At that precise moment, the cube unlocked itself and a fizz of sparkling, white energy rose from it. As the tiny walls fell gracefully apart and the cloud of particles dissipated, the Doctor's mind was filled with the impression of something…

Something…

He couldn't quite articulate the thought in his mind. All he knew was, he had to go to the console. He placed the opened pieces of the cube into his jacket pocket and jumped to his feet. His hands set to work, rapidly adjusting coordinates. The TARDIS was quick to respond, her engines groaning reassuringly. Moments later, they thudded to a halt.

The Doctor breathed a sigh of satisfaction. He patted the console and smiled.

'Clever old thing. Well done.'

He pulled the console's screen towards him, peering at the whirl of symbols and graphics on it. He'd never been here before, he knew that. But he had heard the name of the place.

'The planet Gethria,' he mouthed to himself.

All the readings showed the planet could support a wide range of life forms, so he decided to go outside, pausing only briefly to activate the wall scanner to see what he could expect to be greeted with. He frowned as he saw the barren, desert landscape and some kind of gigantic, ancient stone monument. Hard, grey, granite-like. Just below it, there was a small gathering of humanoids.

'Bound to be friendly,' he muttered, half-suspecting his optimism might be misplaced. But the same kind of compulsion that had led him to set the coordinates for Gethria seemed to be driving him now. He was possessed of a feeling that he couldn't quite understand. He just *knew* he must set foot on this world.

The TARDIS had landed about half a mile away from the monument. This gave the Doctor plenty of time to survey the group of humanoids as he approached over the crumbling, dry surface of Gethria. He made no attempt to hide himself. He could, for example, have darted between rocky outcrops, alternately hiding and dashing for cover; but there was really no need, he thought.

The closer he got to the gathering, the more it became apparent to the Doctor that these people were not the slightest bit interested in anything other than whatever it was directly in front of them. He couldn't see what that was for now; but they were all staring down at it.

As he got ever closer, some indistinct words drifted across to him on the dry, dusty breeze. Although he couldn't quite make them out, they sounded sombre and respectful in tone.

And then, before he had reached the gathering, as if responding to some unspoken signal, the humanoids began to depart, walking slowly, heads bowed, around the monument, heading off in the opposite direction to the Doctor. He felt almost compelled to stop, finding himself instinctively bowing his own head, as if he were attending…

A funeral. That was it. It was a funeral. Yes. The dappled grey of the long, hooded cloaks these people were wearing... That was a popular form of funeral attire in... Oh, somewhere in the universe the Doctor had long forgotten about.

And *there* was the grave. Right where they had all been standing. It had a rather beautiful but stark, engraved, orange headstone – evidently imported from far away. Embedded in the curve of its upper edge were half a dozen small items, encased in glass or something very similar, like fragments of memory caught in clear amber. As with the dappled grey cloaks, the Doctor remembered, the encasing of a person's chosen mementoes in a gravestone was an age-old tradition in many parts of the cosmos.

As the Doctor began to approach the stone for a closer look, he suddenly felt he was being looked at. Twitching a look to the right, he saw one of the mourners.

It was an old lady. She had clearly paused to turn and look at him.

Their eyes met. To the Doctor, it felt like she was waiting for something. A greeting? Recognition? Something... But for the Doctor, there was nothing. He did not know her.

Perhaps she sensed this, it wasn't clear, but after a few seconds, she turned her head away and walked off, following the other mourners at a steady pace, making no attempt to catch up.

Shrugging, the Doctor turned his attention back to the embedded mementoes in glass. He found himself being drawn to what looked like a tiny spaceship. He pushed his face close to the transparent casing around its miniature hull.

'Hmmm,' he mused. 'Anyone at home?'

Crouching, he could see some lettering on the underside of the ship.

'Made in Carthedia,' he read aloud. 'You're a toy, aren't you?' The Doctor grinned his broad grin and ruffled his hair. He chuckled to himself. He knew the difference between a memory and the faint tingle he felt when something from his future was reaching back to him. He knew that sometimes the complexities of time travel meant he had to be patient.

'Something for another day,' he muttered to himself. 'But I shall remember you, little spaceship. I shall remember you.' And he pointed at it, chuckling again, moving closer and closer to the glass. So close now that the little ship started to blur and the microscopic flaws in the transparent 'amber' around it looked like the tracks of eternity, reaching out to tantalise the Doctor.

He snapped back up to his full height, swaying, inelegant, looking up at the giant monument. One day, this would mean something to him, he felt. One day…

But not today.

As the Doctor turned and left the graveside, striding off back to the TARDIS, he was being observed.

Deep within a vast, metallic complex, surging with the power of a terrifying, almost unimaginably superior technology, there seethed the hatred and determination of a single, powerful intellect. Contained within the bonded polycarbide armour of a Dalek, this creature was the result of generations of genetic manipulation. Manipulation with but one aim: to furnish the Dalek race with a controlling force that could see into the frenzied chaos of the Time Vortex and read its unfathomable patterns.

This was the Dalek Time Controller.

The upper grating sections of its casing, just below its dome, were diagonally circled by revolving rings, like the whirling debris fields around a gas giant, appearing solid from a distance, but close up... Close up, they burned with the energy of the Vortex that unfolded in the open gateway in front of this ultimate form of Dalek life.

Its eyestalk twitched, agitatedly, as it followed the image superimposed in the centre of the Vortex. The Doctor was still moving towards his TARDIS on the planet Gethria.

Inside its casing, the mutant body of the Dalek Time Controller quivered with something very like anticipation and delight. Behind it, not daring to approach the open gateway into eternity, a squad of high-ranking Daleks eased a little closer to their soothsayer. They too had spotted the Doctor.

He was now entering the TARDIS. The door closed behind him. A few moments later, the TARDIS groaned the hoarse groan of its temporal engines and was gone.

In a voice infused with an almost exultant, dark determination, more guttural and yet more delicate than any other Dalek's voice, the Time Controller finally spoke.

'It is beginning...'

*

At another, precise point in the infinity of space and time, a young girl was terrified – and it was becoming more and more difficult for her to remember a time when she had not been. She sat, hunched, hugging herself as tight as she could, shivering in spasms of cold and fear so relentless and all-consuming that it felt to her as if the cold and the fear were becoming the same thing.

She squeezed her eyes tight shut again. But all she found in her mind were terrible memories she could almost not bear to think about. She remembered the shouting, running, an explosion... Sheer terror.

There had been a man. He was kind, she had thought. He had rescued her... Her and her little brother.

Her little brother!

She remembered him calling out to her. 'We'll come back for you! We'll come back for you! I promise!'

The thoughts were too painful and she opened her eyes again. The memories faded into the grimy, grey-silver walls of her boxed, featureless cell. She stared at the angles of the walls, followed the lines where they met the low ceiling, looked down to where they met the hard, metallic floor. Not for the first time, she felt the rising panic within her that this would be all she would see for the rest of her life. Seized by the fear of this unending blankness, she found herself cherishing the dim hope that a Dalek might come again to feed her. Just one Dalek with some food. Just something to break through the nothingness.

But there was nothing. Just the low, muffled heartbeat of the Dalek ship's power and the vibration of its engines.

Time flowed past, but she had no way of knowing how fast or slow. Was this just a minute? Or days? Was she a grown-up now? Had she spent her whole life here?

One of the walls suddenly slid to one side, revealing a Dalek behind it. Her heart leapt with anticipation. It was carrying a small tray in its sucker arm. Extending the sucker downwards, it dropped the tray onto the floor. A bowl of something disgusting-looking jumped violently on impact, spilling some of its grey, foul-smelling contents.

In that moment, she caught sight of her distorted reflection in the burnished bronze of the Dalek's armour. The image was dull and warped, but she could see… she was still a little girl. She still had a lifetime of captivity ahead of her.

She started to sob, uncontrollably. Perhaps, she hoped, she would cry her life out and fade away from this horrible ordeal right now. She could almost feel the relief of it all being over.

'Eat!' shrieked the piercing electronic voice of the Dalek. 'Eat!'

It was like a hard slap to her face. The tears dried up and she looked into the bowl. How could she eat *that*? And then she remembered…

Her favourite thing in the whole wide world…

Jelly blobs. Sweet, sweet jelly blobs. So bad for her teeth. But so utterly delicious. If she pretended this food was jelly blobs, she could eat it and the Dalek would stop shrieking.

She reached into the bowl and fished out the imaginary jelly blobs, believing with every bitter,

Chapter Two
Distress Call

Having only recently set the TARDIS to dematerialise from the surface of Gethria, the Doctor was still pondering the mystery of his visit to the lonely funeral on that barren world. He was swinging in a hammock beneath the glass platform upon which the console sat. More and more these days, he found himself gently swinging here, mulling over things as the TARDIS drifted through the Vortex. Was he just becoming a brooding old Doctor in his old age? Or was he finally getting a real sense of perspective?

Launching himself out of the hammock and landing on the pockmarked coral of the control room's lower floor, he tapped his impressive chin... pondering unabated.

So, he was thinking, the cube was definitely from the future, unless he'd somehow mysteriously forgotten something... which was always possible. But how could that've happened?

'Hmmm,' he found himself saying aloud.

He pondered further... Why was the cube so small? Made in a hurry? Possibly, yes. But still... Aha! Yes, the contents. The contents! Nothing too complicated. It was merely filled with an impression of something. And which species was mostly capable of mere telepathic impressions rather than complex telepathic messages? Humans! Of course!

He reached his conclusion... At some point in the future, he was going to make this simplified telepathic cube for a human to use.

Of course! Clever Doctor.

But then, he realised, he still had no idea why he was going to do this.

'That's the future for you,' he concluded, dashing up the steps to his beloved console. He gazed at the controls in joyous anticipation. Even when nothing made sense and the future was a frustrating fog, the sheer beauty and ingenuity of the TARDIS always made him feel happy to be alive. Perhaps he would just head off somewhere nice and quiet to savour that thought – keep out of trouble.

Suddenly, however, the TARDIS appeared to have other ideas. The console scanner screen was flashing with fragmented images fighting with signal interference. There was the piercing sound of hissing static and the buzzing, electronic contortions of frequency modulation. Someone was trying to get in touch.

Rapidly flicking controls and tapping the side of the screen, the Doctor attempted to clarify the signal – but then it suddenly shut off. For a moment, he pouted in defeat. The TARDIS was always passing through so many different possible destinations, it was almost inevitable that it would fly past one discrete transmission without any hope of finding it again... even if he managed to throw everything into reverse.

Nevertheless, he tried it. The control room shuddered violently, and smoke started seeping from the cracks in the console as the Doctor rapidly pulled levers and twisted dials. The engines groaned and creaked. Everything was juddering as if he had performed a handbrake turn in a vehicle far too frail to survive it.

Continuing with his rapid, emergency adjustments, the Doctor craned his neck to see if anything of the transmission had returned to the scanner... And there it was!

Or rather, there *the man* was. A desperate face, pleading, close up into the transmitter's lens; his mouth distorting with silent anguish.

'Sound, sound, sound!' burbled the Doctor. 'Got to get some sound on that picture!'

Satisfied that the TARDIS had now halted and was drifting back in time and space to the point where the signal had originated, the Doctor jabbed at some buttons. After each jab, he waited a second or two for a result. Nothing. Nothing. And more nothing. He glanced back at the face on the screen. The man was middle-aged and looked extremely upset. Like this was perhaps the worst moment of his life. The Doctor caught sight of a woman behind him. She was frantically busy operating controls.

'Spaceship controls!' the Doctor declared aloud. In

that instant, he knew these were people in trouble in a spaceship, calling desperately for help.

Flipping open the panel on which his recently pushed buttons were situated, the Doctor saw, with a growl of frustration, that some of the wiring had become disconnected. Bits of the TARDIS were always going well past their sell-by date. It was a nightmare trying to keep up with it. Instantly, he grabbed the wires and shoved them into the connectors beneath them. There was a fizz and a pop and a blinding light... and suddenly there was sound from the transmission.

'I repeat!' the terrified voice of the man was saying. 'This is Terrin Blakely. Our coordinates are embedded in this transmission! We need help, urgently! We are under attack! We— It's no good, Alyst!'

Terrin turned his back to the lens. The Doctor moved closer to the screen, his hands dancing across more controls. He was setting about reading the embedded coordinates. Something terrible was happening aboard this Terrin chap's spaceship, but the Doctor couldn't precisely see what – and then the transmission broke off in a fierce crackle of static. The screen was dead.

'Don't worry, Terrin,' said the Doctor, isolating the coordinates in the transmission stream. 'I'll be there before you know it. Before you even sent the signal, if I get this right!'

And, triumphantly, the Doctor set the TARDIS in motion again. He had set a clear course right back to what he hoped were a few moments before Terrin made the call.

*

Deep within its gigantic command ship, the Dalek Time Controller twitched its appendages with instinctive delight as its eye lens narrowed on the image of the Doctor in his TARDIS. Satisfied that the time was right for drastic intervention, the Time Controller swivelled its dome 180 degrees so that its eyestalk faced the assembled Dalek hierarchy to the rear of it.

'It is time,' its voice growled in a fusion of guttural determination and electronic detachment. 'One energy pulse, aimed at those precise space-time coordinates!'

One of the assembled Daleks recognised its area of responsibility and instantly responded.

'I obey!'

It reversed, then glided to a control panel, quickly and efficiently, its sucker arm immediately attaching to a circular socket. A command impulse was instantly sent into the Dalek Time Control ship's weaponry systems.

With a gigantic shudder, a precisely aimed energy pulse was fired into the Vortex.

Just as the TARDIS engines were engaging for materialisation on board Terrin Blakely's ship, some huge, destructive force smashed into the ancient time ship. The control room seemed to flip upside down for a moment, and the Doctor had to hold on to a couple of levers to stop himself crashing downwards into the high ceiling. Hot sparks sprayed from every power outlet and ten or more dials exploded and melted.

'This is sheer vandalism!' cried the Doctor over the terrible din that engulfed the control room. He crashed back down to the floor as the TARDIS righted itself. Whatever had hit now faded away and the ship completed its materialisation.

Staggering to his feet, the Doctor patted the console affectionately. 'You clever, sexy thing,' he whispered, still gasping from being winded by the shock of impact.

The TARDIS engines came to a halt as the ship landed. Activating the wall scanner, the Doctor felt a pang of worry. All he could see was the empty control room of Terrin's spaceship. No signs of life. The atmosphere checked out as stale but breathable. Without further hesitation, the Doctor rushed to the door and stepped out.

Terrin Blakely's ship was functional and unimpressive. All its control surfaces were well worn and the furnishings looked a bit tired. The metal deck was scuffed with what looked like decades of footsteps. This was an old workhorse of a ship, probably hired out to anyone and everyone – no careful owners.

'You chartered this old bucket of bolts, Terrin,' muttered the Doctor to himself as he flipped a few controls. There was a gentle, unhealthy sizzling sound emitting from the panels.

'Terrin!' called the Doctor. 'Terrin, are you here?'

The Doctor's words echoed a truncated echo into the dull, greenish walls. Fishing his sonic screwdriver from his pocket, he took various readings as he made a quick dash around the length and breadth of the ship. It took him just a few minutes. There was a main, central corridor, off which fanned a number of cabins with bunks in. At the head of the corridor was this oval-shaped control room, at the rear was a rectangular engine section, where the display panels were also sizzling and smoking.

The readings in the control room showed that the ship had indeed been attacked. Attempts at generating a defensive energy field around the ship had failed, and there were a few fresh scorch marks here and there, some still wet with foam, where fires had broken out and been extinguished. The Doctor's nostrils twitched with the still-present sting of burnt plastic and scorched metal.

'So, where are you?' asked the Doctor of the empty spaces he imagined that Terrin had once occupied. 'What happened to you, Terrin, old chap? And that lady? Was it your wife? Hmm. I wonder…'

The Doctor's eyes darted over the controls. There was still some power. With some careful re-routing, things would still work.

'Aha!'

He located something he knew might help.

It was the log recorder… That should answer a few questions, he thought as he approached a small screen with a camera lens fitted above it.

After a few false starts, the Doctor found the correct way to get this recorder to display the contents of its electronic memory. He punched a sequence of buttons and the screen spluttered into life, almost spitting out static with sharp needles of distorted sound.

And the tragedy unfolded before his eyes…

The moment the gigantic ship had arrived in front of them, blocking their course, Terrin had been prepared. He activated the log recorder and was ready to send a distress call as soon as the alien aggressors made their first demand.

Alyst had seen a look in his eyes that she had never seen before in all their seventeen years of marriage, and it scared her. Ever since they had agreed to set out on this voyage, she had had the distinct feeling that their work had taken them a step too far towards something forbidden and dangerous. And now she knew it was true.

Terrin was violently hammering a release control for the ship's escape pod. Alyst had never seen him do anything remotely violent before, but now he was attacking this control with an unrestrained, almost animalistic brute force. The control still did not respond.

'It's not going to work,' Terrin said. 'This damn ship! Nothing on it works properly! No self-destruct and now no escape pod!'

Alyst realised what would have to happen.

The communications speaker crackled into life again. It was that Dalek again, making its blunt demand.

'You will surrender the formula immediately!'

Alyst saw Terrin's fear fire his anger as he hit the response button.

'I've already told you! We don't know what you are talking about,' he said, desperately, clearly not believing his own words.

'We know you are lying,' the Dalek stated. 'We know you have been in correspondence with Hogoosta on Gethria. We know you have the formula! You will surrender it immediately. We will now board your ship.'

'You won't find the formula here!' shouted Terrin.

'You are lying,' the Dalek responded. 'Prepare to be boarded.'

'I'm not lying!' screamed Terrin back to the crackling speaker.

Alyst felt herself compelled to move to her husband. She gripped his arm, as if their being together might make all this go away.

'It's in here, you see!' shouted Terrin, pointing to his head. 'Nowhere else! It's all in here! And I won't be here when you board.'

He cut off the communications and tried to pull away from Alyst. She thought of saying 'no', but she knew there was no point. Even though she had never seen her husband so distressed, so terrified, she knew that he was a man of great purpose and determination. But she still couldn't find it in herself to let go of his arm.

He pulled away from her again and headed towards the airlock.

'Terrin...' she began to say.

'No,' he said simply, not even turning. 'I won't talk about it. You know I love you. You know I have to do this.'

'I'm coming with—' she started.

'No!' And she saw the angry pain on his face as he turned. 'You don't know the formula!'

'But I know enough,' she said. She could see that he knew she was right. 'I know too much.'

Without another word, she moved to his side and they both walked towards the airlock, their hands linking tightly.

*

The Doctor turned away from the playback as he heard the sound of the airlock discharging Terrin and Alyst into space. He felt a hollowness somewhere inside him. The same feeling he always had when the Daleks crossed his path. Their capacity to surprise and outrage him with their repetitive acts of inhumanity filled him with a rage that he always hoped against hope would diminish over time. But here he was again, starting to learn of yet another Dalek plan for conquest or destruction or invasion or whatever mad, bad idea they had in mind... And he was gritting his teeth in silent fury.

The Dalek capacity to cause suffering and death seemed boundless to the Doctor. He had witnessed their birth in the fires of war, fought them across eternity, tasted their cruelty at first hand so many times. He might have expected his feelings to be blunted to their effect. Yet, witnessing two people who clearly loved each other sacrifice their lives rather than fall captive to the Daleks made the Doctor's anger and despair as keen as ever it had been.

A tear started to form in his left eye, but he blinked it away. They would not have that from him. He would shed no more tears over the horrors the Daleks could inflict. He would not give them the satisfaction.

'Formula, formula, formula,' the Doctor muttered to himself, feverishly. Already his mind was focusing on the problem in hand. No laments for the dead. He mustn't waste time on anger. He must simply defeat them.

'What was this formula, eh, Terrin?' he mused, moving to the airlock. He looked through the inner door window. The outer door was still open to the freezing blackness of space. He hammered home the door control, closing it and re-pressurising the airlock with a gushing hiss of oxygen. 'What was so important about it that you opted to end your lives out there?'

He gazed into space. No sign of their bodies. No sign of the Dalek ship. All was quiet. Whatever had hit the TARDIS had pushed him some way off course. Why?

'And why didn't the Daleks board your ship, even after you'd gone?' he asked himself. 'Just to make sure. Not like the Daleks *not* to make sure. Why aren't they still here?'

The words froze on his lips, as cold as space, as a distinct sound punctured the stale air. The hairs on the back of the Doctor's neck were all standing on end. For a split second, he dared not turn round.

And there was the noise again. It was a shifting, groaning sound, some way off. It was coming from the rear of the ship. The engine room? Was there a Dalek in the engine room?

It struck the Doctor as faintly ridiculous that he was now starting to tiptoe, given that, a few moments ago, he had been shouting and thundering around the ship as fast as his lanky legs could carry him in such a confined space – but his instincts had taken over. He approached the rear of the ship as quietly as he could.

The noise came again. Shifting again, like something... *slithering* across metal. Then a bump echoed through the hull. Bumping, slithering, shifting? Not the sort of sounds he readily associated with Daleks. He stopped and dared to take a reading with his sonic screwdriver. It buzzed gently to itself and the Doctor glanced down to interpret its findings. There was nothing in them that indicated the presence of a Dalek.

'Hello!' the Doctor dared to call out. 'Who's there?'

After a few moments of silence, in which the low hum of the ship's faltering power and the worrying sizzling seemed to get unpleasantly louder, there was a different sound. Muted and indistinct, it was definitely vocal and followed by a 'ssssh' noise.

Someone was 'sssshing' someone! Someone was *hiding*. And more than one someone, at that. For someone to be 'sssshing', there had to be someone else making the noise to be 'sssshed' in the first place…

Boldly, the Doctor strode forward to the engine room door, pulled it open, paying no heed to its screeching, rusty hinges, and stepped in. He looked around the small, rectangular room, aware that he had clearly missed something when he had looked in here earlier. Then he spotted it, obscured by the rising fumes and dim lighting. A wide panel with steps leading up to it and handles either side. Across the middle of the panel were stencilled faded, fragmented words:

ESCAPE POD

It was the pod that, on the log recording, Terrin had said was not working; and yet now, there was clearly someone in it.

'Terrin?' called the Doctor, his face close to the door panel. 'Are you in there?'

There was no response. If it was Terrin and his wife in

there, the Doctor reasoned, they would surely answer. They had called for help, after all. So, why would there be people in an escape pod who wouldn't answer to someone who had responded to their distress call?

All at once, a string of ideas hit the Doctor. It would be people who had been *told* to keep quiet, no matter what. People who, despite being told to keep quiet, might fidget and 'ssssh' each other. A particular kind of 'people'…

The Doctor grasped the handles and wrenched the panel open.

'Children!' he announced, as he stared down at three cowering figures, blinking and cringing in the meagre, flickering light of the engine room. And these children had been cramped together in the dark for…

'How long have you been here?' asked the Doctor.

All three of them looked scared to death. The Doctor smiled at them, reassuringly, but they seemed impervious to reassurance. So he stepped back and waited for a while, until they stopped squinting and blinking. He realised that he must have initially just looked like an enormous, blurred silhouette to them.

Hoping they could now see him a bit more clearly, he smiled again and straightened his bow tie. The smaller child in the middle, a boy, shifted a little and nuzzled into the other two, both girls, almost certainly a bit older, definitely a bit bigger.

'Er, I'm not very good at children's ages,' said the Doctor, consciously making his face a picture of innocence. He pointed to the boy. 'You'd be about… oooh, 32 years old, am I right?'

The little boy immediately giggled. The girl on his left, with blonde curly hair, squeezed a protective arm around him. She frowned an angry frown.

'Older than that?' asked the Doctor, trying to provoke another giggle. The girl on the left squeezed the boy tighter and the other girl, on the right, with dark, straight hair, put a protective arm around him too, now.

'I did a wee in my pants,' said the boy in the tiniest of voices. The girls instantly 'sssshed' him together.

'Oh. Well, I'm not surprised,' said the Doctor, conversationally. 'I expect you've been in there quite a long time. I expect if I'd been in there all that time, I would have done a wee in my pants too.'

The Doctor flicked the braces on his trousers and pulled at the waist, miming being uncomfortable and making an 'Urrrrgh' noise.

'Where's Mummy and Daddy?' asked the blonde girl. It sounded more like an accusation.

The Doctor felt sick inside. He didn't know what to say. And looking at the children's eyes didn't help him. He could see that the eldest girl, the blonde one, suspected that something terrible had happened. The dark-haired girl seemed more confused. The boy appeared to be mostly concerned about his own discomfort. He wriggled, screwing up his face, and the eldest girl gave him a tiny slap.

'No hitting,' the little boy said.

'They're dead, aren't they?' said the blonde girl directly at the Doctor.

All the Doctor could do was nod, slowly. The blonde girl's eyes seemed at once afire with anger, filling with tears. She just stared at the Doctor, almost unblinking as the tears dribbled silently down her face. The other, dark-haired girl was watching her, unsure.

'Sabel?' she asked of the blonde girl. 'Sabel, where are they?'

'They're dead, Jeni,' said Sabel, coldly. She tried to say it again, but her voice faltered into a whisper, trailing off. 'They're…' and she swallowed, uncomfortably, not taking her eyes off the Doctor for one instant.

The little boy wriggled again. 'I need to change my pants,' he said.

'I'm…' the Doctor started. He wanted to say he was very sorry, but it sounded so pointless. Then, he said it anyway. 'I'm very sorry.'

The one Sabel had called Jeni turned to the Doctor now, looking angry too. 'Did you kill them?'

'No,' said the Doctor, calmly. 'No, I didn't.'

'It was the Daleks, wasn't it?' said Sabel. 'The Daleks wanted the formula and Daddy wouldn't give it to them.'

'What formula?' asked the Doctor.

'I really need to change my pants!' the boy suddenly blurted out loudly.

'Why don't you take him to his room and help him change his pants?' the Doctor asked the girls. He stepped forward to offer them a hand out of the pod.

'Keep back,' said Sabel, sharply. 'We don't need your help. We can manage.'

The Doctor backed away, then thought it best if he left them alone for a while. He turned and walked back to the control room. He could hear their footsteps behind him, as they clambered out of the pod and walked along the corridor. He turned and saw them disappear into one of the small cabins.

He waited patiently in the control room. For what seemed a long time, he stood perfectly still, staring out of the forward view-port, at the nothingness of space. There were Daleks out there, somewhere. There always were, of course, but once again, they had made it personal. Their latest scheme had caused a tragedy to unfold before him. They had crossed his path like an ancient omen of bad fortune, and now it felt to him almost as if he must heave on his battle-stained armour again to fight them.

His thoughts were broken by the sound of the children crying, coming from the cabin back down the corridor. It sounded as if Sabel had finally made it clear to what he was sure was her little brother that his mother and father were dead. The Doctor could pick out Sabel's low, faltering voice. It was Jeni and the boy who were crying.

Listening harder, the Doctor could even discern some of Sabel's words as she spoke firmly and with more purpose.

'You mustn't cry any more, Ollus… Jenibeth. You mustn't cry. We must all be brave. It's what Mummy and Daddy would have wanted.'

'But what shall we do now?' came Jeni's voice.

There was a pause. Sabel clearly didn't have a plan. Who could blame her? She was probably only about 8 years old.

'Will the funny man look after us?' came Ollus's tiny voice.

The Funny Man? thought the Doctor. Well, if he could at least be that for them, he might bring some light into their lives to help them through the terrible pain they must be feeling. He might at least do that, to make up for the heartache the Daleks had wrought here.

Deciding not to eavesdrop any more, the Doctor sniffed back his emotions and concentrated on the controls of the ship. A cursory examination confirmed to him that although it was damaged, it was space-worthy. He could, perhaps, take the children home without subjecting them to the disorientation of travelling in the TARDIS.

He was suddenly aware of the shuffle of little footsteps behind him. He turned and saw the children, assembled in a line, holding hands. Ollus, the little boy in the middle, between his two sisters again, stumbled back, slightly overawed, and the girls were forced to stumble back with him. Sabel pulled all three forward again. She really was the brave one.

'So…' said the Doctor, a bit lost for words. He smiled as reassuringly as he could and crouched down, to make himself less imposing for them. He looked at Ollus. 'All better, then?'

Ollus nodded and unintentionally pulled Jeni's hand over his face as he attempted to scratch his nose. Jeni tutted, irritated, and yanked his arm back.

'Ollus!' she hissed, disapprovingly.

'So…' started the Doctor again, still unsure quite how to treat the children. 'I thought I'd take you all back home.'

The children looked at him, blankly.

'There's probably someone back home, isn't there?' asked the Doctor. 'Someone who could look after you all?'

Still, they said nothing.

'OK…' said the Doctor. 'Well, I'm sure there'll be someone. Um… can you tell me where you're from?'

Still nothing.

'Anyone? Come on. You must know where you're from.'

Finally, Sabel spoke. 'Will the Daleks come back?'

And the Doctor realised that his reassuring tone counted for absolutely nothing. How could he honestly tell them the Daleks wouldn't come back? They always came back.

'Well,' he finally decided. 'They might do. Yes. Yes. They might do. Which is why we have to get you back home, where it's safe…' he trailed off. 'Hopefully safe… in case the Daleks do… er… do come back here.'

'There isn't anyone who could look after us,' said Sabel.

'Not even an aunt or an uncle?' asked the Doctor. 'Or a grandmother or grandfather?'

'No,' said Sabel.

'Oh,' said the Doctor. 'Well, I'm… I'm sure there'll be… er… well, someone…' He trailed off again, turning his back on them, wincing to himself, feeling totally incompetent, as he approached the astro-navigation section of the controls. Tapping a few keys, he brought up a display showing a star chart.

'Now then… Local space,' he muttered to himself. He was looking for their most likely point of origin.

As he pushed his finger around the screen, planetary symbols popped out like rapidly inflating, 3-D balloons, text detailing their names, population, mass, and other information scrolling underneath.

All of a sudden, the Doctor was aware of tiny footsteps rushing towards him.

'Ollus!' called Sabel, scoldingly. But Ollus was already heading straight for the Doctor, arm outstretched, a strange, nasal noise emanating from him.

'Neeeeeeeeeooooowwww!' he intoned.

The Doctor almost gasped out loud when he saw what little Ollus was holding in his outstretched hand. It was a tiny toy spaceship.

Ollus made a huge, splashy impact sound with his mouth as he brought the tiny toy into contact with the screen on a planetary symbol named 'Carthedia'. The Doctor realised that Ollus was approximating the noise of retro rockets firing.

The scrolling text read: 'Carthedia. Earth Alliance colony planet. Total population: 3 billion...'

Satisfied his spaceship had landed and having finished his retro-roaring, Ollus turned to the Doctor and smiled. His smile lit up the Doctor's face.

'Carthedia!' announced Ollus.

'That's your home?' asked the Doctor. 'Carthedia?'

'Yes,' said Ollus.

'You can read?' asked the Doctor. 'You seem too young to be able to read.'

'He's the clever one,' explained Jenibeth. 'We're all quite clever, actually. But Ollus is especially clever. That's what Daddy says... er, said...' Her head suddenly bowed. The Doctor moved to put a hand on her shoulder, but Sabel pulled her away. The Doctor nodded, understanding.

'Well, er… Well done, Ollus,' said the Doctor. 'Do you mind if I have a little look at your spaceship?'

Ollus snatched it away and hid it in his right-hand trouser pocket. He shook his head.

'Oh, all right then,' said the Doctor. But even without a closer examination, he was sure that the little spaceship was the same one he had seen embedded in glass on the head of that gravestone on Gethria. 'Made in Carthedia', the tiny inscription on it had read.

And the Doctor knew that he had already been to this little boy's funeral.

Chapter Three
Return to Carthedia

It would take some time for this tired old ship to make the voyage back to Carthedia. Whatever had happened during the Dalek attack on the vessel had made its power cells very unstable, so the Doctor dared not risk setting it to maximum velocity. As he watched the various monitor screens, constantly making sure everything was running safely, he idly wondered whether the Daleks had fired on the ship at all. Thinking about the damage he had seen, it occurred to him that such minor harm to the ship had merely been caused by the Blakelys' attempts at setting up a defence screen. Furthermore, whether the Dalek ship had fired or not in this encounter, they must have seen Terrin and his wife eject themselves into space. And if that were the case, why, then, had the Daleks not destroyed the spaceship?

'Not like the Daleks...' muttered the Doctor, realising instantly that he had said this only a few hours before. Something odd was going on. The Daleks were behaving... oddly. 'What are you up to, eh?' he said.

'Who are you talking to?'

Sabel had pulled up another well-worn fold-out swivel chair to sit next to where the Doctor was already reclining, with his pointy boots on the control panel. He instantly sat up, putting his feet down on the floor, as if he had been told off.

Sabel looked at him, not as fiercely as before. But she still clearly didn't trust him.

'Oh…' said the Doctor, in the absence of any coherent, acceptable response occurring to him. Then he opted for the truth. 'I was talking to myself, actually,' he said, smiling warmly. The warmth was not returned.

'How did you get on board our ship and what's that big blue crate over there?' asked Sabel, nodding towards the TARDIS.

'That's how I got on board your ship,' smiled the Doctor. 'It's the TARDIS.'

Sabel regarded the TARDIS for a moment. She clearly did not believe him.

'Seriously,' said the Doctor, a little hurt.

Sabel turned to look out of the view-port, apparently not interested in talking to the Doctor any more. He felt a little dismissed. He swivelled his chair around, absently. Ollus was sitting on the deck by the door, engrossed in playing with his spaceship toy. It was quite a technologically impressive little item, thought the Doctor, and Ollus was very adept at 'operating' it.

Accompanied by an array of fizzing and buzzing sounds, the toy ship flashed various colours and projected tiny holographic images around its hull – whooshing space warps, cascading comets, gigantic planets, some orange, some blue, some coloured like pulsing rainbows. There were moments when the ship itself even seemed to hover a little, or perhaps the Doctor was mistaken about that.

Jenibeth emerged from a cabin somewhere down the corridor. She was carrying a small, plastic packet of something. As she walked along, she was staring into it with fervent determination, totally absorbed. Whatever she was about to fish out, speculated the Doctor, it seemed as though it was going to be her favourite thing.

With a resolute crackle of plastic, Jenibeth finally pulled out a small, bright green blob of something. She held it up for a moment, admiring it. Then she licked it with delight and popped it into her mouth, instantly chewing, her cheeks bunching in a grin of pure joy. The Doctor thought of telling her that sweets would rot her teeth, but he stopped himself, remembering that these children needed all the happiness in their lives they could find.

He swivelled his chair back to view the control panels and read-out screens. Everything was still working well, although the power levels were far from ideal. He glanced back at Sabel. She was still staring ahead.

'This formula,' the Doctor said to her. 'Have you any idea what sort of thing it was?'

Sabel continued to stare ahead. 'A secret.'

'A secret the Daleks wanted to get hold of,' said the Doctor. 'So it must be something bad.'

'Why?' asked Sabel.

'Because everything the Daleks do is bad,' said the Doctor.

To his surprise, Sabel seemed genuinely curious. She reached out a foot and propelled her chair round to face him. The Doctor swivelled to face her too. He was intrigued.

'You know what the Daleks are?' he asked.

'Yes,' said Sabel. 'They help people.'

'Help people?' the Doctor was appalled. 'What do you mean by that?'

'The Sunlight Worlds. They made those, didn't they?'

'The Sunlight...? Did they?' asked the Doctor. 'Actually, I don't care what they've made, it always leads to the most terrible trouble. That's what you've got to remember about the Da—' He suddenly cut himself short. 'Wait a minute! Did your father think the Daleks "help people"?'

Sabel seemed confused about the Doctor's question. 'Of course. Everyone knows that.'

'Then why didn't he just give them this formula of his, if he thought the Daleks were apparently so nice?' asked the Doctor.

'Because Hogoosta said no one must ever know about the formula, that's why,' said Sabel, simply. 'No one at all. Ever.'

'Why not?' The Doctor decided to ask about this 'Hogoosta' later.

'Because he said it was dangerous and no one must know about it,' she said, rather unhelpfully.

'So, how come *you* know about it?' asked the Doctor.

'I don't really,' confessed Sabel. 'I just heard Mummy and Daddy talking about it. And even if I did know, I couldn't tell you about it anyway. I mean, who are you?'

'I'm the Doctor,' the Doctor said, simply, as if that explained everything. He thought he might just get away with that.

'Did you know my Mummy or Daddy?' Sabel asked, almost hopefully, as if his knowing them might mean a little of them was still alive.

The Doctor didn't like disappointing Sabel. 'Er… well, no, I didn't. But I'd *like* to know about them. About what they did and who this Hogoosta person was.'

Sabel considered for a moment. The Doctor was encouraged that it really did seem as though he may actually have got away with not explaining who he was.

Suddenly, Ollus spoke, without looking up from his toy. 'Hogoosta looked funny. He made me laugh.'

'Did he?' asked the Doctor, grateful for the change of focus. 'What was funny about him?'

'He had lots of legs,' said Jenibeth, through a mouthful of her chewy green blob. 'And he went *scuttle-scuttle-scuttle*, like that.' She made a spider-like walking motion with her hands.

'He wasn't human, you mean?' asked the Doctor.

'He's from Gethria,' explained Sabel. 'You don't know him?'

'Er… no,' confessed the Doctor. 'But, um… I've *been* to Gethria. Although, possibly not… er… recently.' He thought back to the funeral he had witnessed. About the little spaceship in the gravestone. He looked at Ollus, engrossed with that spaceship, staring with wonder through its multicoloured, holographic projections.

'So how did this Hogoosta… person… How did he know your parents?' asked the Doctor.

The Doctor positioned his chair so that he could see all three children, and patiently listened as they started revealing fragments of a fascinating and disturbing account. He learnt that their parents, Terrin and Alyst, were highly thought of physicists and polymaths. It was clear that their influence had been passed down to Sabel, Jenibeth and Ollus too… especially Ollus, who seemed capable of really quite breathtakingly sophisticated thought processes for a boy who was, the Doctor learnt, not yet 5 years old.

Apparently ever interested in expanding their knowledge, Terrin and Alyst, the Doctor was told, had begun a long-distance correspondence course with an esteemed Klektid archaeologist on the planet Gethria. As he listened to the unfolding story, the Doctor set part of his mind to work on recalling exactly what a Klektid was.

Hogoosta's work was concerned with the unearthing of an ancient monument, known to be called the 'Cradle of the Gods' – no one knew why, apparently. Terrin and Alyst had freely participated in an 'exchange of knowledge' programme, sharing much of it with their children. Sabel, Jenibeth and Ollus had been shown many images of this Cradle of the Gods. They had found it fascinating. What the Doctor found more fascinating, however, was that their descriptions of it began to conjure up an image in his mind of the giant, granite-like structure *he* had seen on Gethria.

In return for giving the ever knowledge-hungry Blakelys a crash course in archaeology, Hogoosta had been taught more and more about physics by them.

Ollus, who loved talking about Hogoosta and his 'funny, bony legs', was keen to tell the Doctor as much as he could. The Doctor was grateful enough, although, despite being impressed at how advanced for his age Ollus seemed, he still wished that perhaps one of the older children had helped with the narrative at this point.

'He sended things to Mummy and Daddy and they liked them, cos they thought those were good pictures, so they sended good pictures back to Hogoosta-funny-legs and they said he was smiling, but his mouths was so bony and funny that I couldn't see a smile, but Hogoosta-funny-legs said he was happy, he used to talk to me and show me funny old things made of stone that were good and made me laugh a lot.'

The Doctor tried to stay focused. 'And... er... that's good, Ollus. That's good. Er... but what *were* these pictures?'

'Pictures and funny letters and numbers and things that Daddy said were numbers but were not like I sawed before, cos they were on stone and not like our letters or numbers, they weren't.' Ollus stared intently at the Doctor, as if this explained everything.

Complex equations of some sort, thought the Doctor. That's what Ollus was talking about. Hogoosta was sending Terrin and Alyst complex equations 'on stone'. Equations Hogoosta had found somewhere on this Cradle of the Gods monument, perhaps.

Much to the Doctor's relief, Sabel picked up the story. She explained that her parents suddenly became unhappy. Things had been going so well between them and Hogoosta, but now she heard them arguing with the Klektid archaeologist over the interplanetary comms screen. Sabel had heard that something her parents had sent back to Hogoosta in response to one of these equations on stone had proved to be 'dangerous' in some way. Hogoosta had told Terrin and Alyst to destroy all record of it. He said that no one must know of whatever it was.

'But your father already had it in his head, didn't he?' asked the Doctor. 'So... Hogoosta wanted him to come to Gethria, didn't he?'

'Yes,' Jenibeth said, through another mouthful of blobby sweets. 'But Mummy wouldn't let him go. She said that we must all go together. Mummy and Daddy loved each other lots, you see.'

'Yes, yes... of course they did,' said the Doctor quietly, feeling sad that such a strong emotional bond had led to such a terrible outcome. 'And they loved you very much, didn't they? They couldn't leave you behind.'

Sabel nodded, a little teary now. 'She said the Blakelys must stick together.'

'Yes... yes, of course...' the Doctor murmured, almost to himself, because he felt his anger at the Daleks rising again. But anger was no good for these poor children and their loss. He forced his mind to focus on clarifying what had happened.

'So your Mummy and Daddy solved some ancient problem, and it turned out to be something more dangerous than this Hogoosta funny-legs chap had ever anticipated, otherwise he wouldn't have spoken about it on an open comms line in the first place,' said the Doctor, in one continuous breath, feeling he was on the trail of something definite.

Ollus was playing with his spaceship again. Jenibeth ate the last of her blobby things, noisily. But Sabel had fixed the Doctor with a look. She was old enough to grasp what he was saying.

'And the Daleks wanted this dangerous thing,' she said, reasoning it out. 'Because… they're bad?'

'Yes, yes, yes,' said the Doctor. 'The Daleks do everything because they're bad.'

And it must have been a pretty bad thing that Terrin had in his head, thought the Doctor, for him to leave his children behind and commit suicide with his wife. Terrin had, the Doctor realised, hoped to jettison the children to safety and destroy the ship, with him on board; but when the self-destruct *and* escape pod hadn't worked, he'd opted to sacrifice his life through the airlock, then hoping to leave his wife alive. But although Alyst may not have known this 'formula', she knew enough about it for that knowledge to prove too useful to the Daleks. So she had sacrificed herself too.

There was one consolation in all this, thought the Doctor. At least the Daleks hadn't managed to get hold of this knowledge. However, even though Terrin and Alyst had apparently come from a world that thought of the Daleks as people who helped others, Terrin had been sufficiently convinced of the terrible risk of letting even a supposedly benevolent race get hold of his secret that he had been prepared to die – and let the secret die with him.

This secret, the Doctor pondered, whatever it was, must have been something truly terrifying. Terrifying enough for a mother and father to leave their cherished children to an uncertain fate... but a fate which at least offered them some hope of life.

He knew also that this would be just the beginning of it all for the Daleks. If they had set their sights on getting hold of this secret formula, for whatever purpose, they weren't going to give up easily. The Doctor knew that, inevitably, he had to try to stop them, no matter what the cost.

When the planetary defence satellites of Carthedia picked up an unidentified craft, whose pilot apparently refused to make contact, initially the government gave an order to scramble an attack force of three orbital fighter craft. But as they approached, the pilot of the unidentified ship finally broke comms silence, explaining that the ship's transmitter had been malfunctioning, 'like most of the rest of the ship', and that he had only just managed to fix it. He further explained that he was bringing three children home. Three children whose parents, Terrin and Alyst Blakely, had sadly died during an 'attack' on their spacecraft as they travelled to the planet Gethria.

This piece of information sent shockwaves around the Carthedia holo-TV media. Three days previously, they had reported on the loss of this very ship. An unidentified freighter captain had given testimony to the effect that a ship chartered by Terrin and Alyst Blakely, to take them and their children to Gethria, had been found, drifting in space, the entire family dead, as a result of an engine malfunction.

So, for those in front of the cameras of the breakfast news bulletin, when this ship entered Carthedia's atmosphere and headed for the capital city's central landing pad, it was like they were presenting a live broadcast of the return of a ghost ship.

'Back from the dead,' proclaimed the newsreaders as their main headline that day.

When the ship finally touched down, the news media were out in force.

In the control room of the ship, the Doctor was screaming. The ship was vibrating like it was the end of the world, every circuit seemed to be blowing and anything not welded to the spot was rattling, crashing and smashing to the deck.

'Geeeerrronimoooooooooooo!'

He locked the landing controls into their final sequence, with the retros firing at full blast, thundering like the raging, opening jaws of hell. There was nothing helpful he could do now to assist the landing, so he spun his chair round so that he could check all three children were still safely strapped into their chairs.

They were. Thank goodness.

It was so clear now, thought the Doctor, that Sabel was the most grown up, because she was aware enough to be terrified – but she was trying to hide it. Ollus was almost completely oblivious to what felt more like a slow motion crash than a landing. He was still managing to play with his tiny spaceship toy, seemingly irritated by the distraction the shaking ship was causing. Jenibeth had found another bag of jelly blobs and was far more interested in cramming the sweets into her mouth than any impending prospects of death.

The Doctor gave them all a desperately optimistic thumbs-up signal. For a moment, Sabel managed the smallest of smiles. Then the ship crunched onto its landing struts... at least that's what the Doctor hoped had caused the gigantic crashing noise, the automatic cut-off of the retros and the sudden, shocking silence.

He froze for a moment, checking for that awful feeling of free fall that might have signalled that the landing rockets had cut off too early, leaving them plunging to certain destruction. But no, he was sure they had landed. All was still.

The Doctor allowed himself a long, outward breath, realising in the process just how much of a breath he'd been holding in... and for how long.

There were only a few creaks of the hull settling now, and the odd spark of control panels and systems that would, hopefully, never see service again.

'We've arrived,' the Doctor managed to murmur through his dry throat. Then he gave the children his biggest smile, putting his thumbs up again.

Allowing the Doctor only the smallest nod of acknowledgement, Sabel quietly released her safety buckles and jumped down from her chair. She trotted straight across to Ollus and Jenibeth, unlocking their buckles for them and taking them by the hand.

The Doctor looked on as they formed their familiar little formation, with Ollus in the middle, this time trying to pull away to play with his spaceship.

'Put it away for now, Ollus,' hissed Sabel.

The Doctor wondered what kind of homecoming this was really going to be for the children. Who would look after them now? Releasing his buckles and standing, he suddenly became aware of an unexpected noise. He cocked an ear. The children had heard it too.

There was a low rumbling sound. Almost like a muted, constant roar. No... not quite constant... It wavered up and down a little.

'OK, anyone know what that is?' asked the Doctor. 'I mean, is it normal for your planet?'

The children had no answers.

The Doctor ran to the main airlock door. For a moment, he felt a little strange about the prospect of passing through this exit. This, after all, had been where Terrin and Alyst had ended their lives. But he pressed on.

Tapping a few keys, he was able to read the atmosphere outside. Nothing odd about it. It could easily sustain human life. Then, before he could do anything more, the opening mechanisms of the door started to crash and moan into place. All at once, the outer door began yawning open of its own accord.

Someone was opening it from the outside, overriding the internal controls. Instinctively, the Doctor stepped back, putting out his hands to protect the children, who were caught in squinting awe as the inner door unsealed, giving way to a penetrating shaft of...

Fresh daylight streamed in. Fresh, bright, fragrant daylight. For a moment, it seemed so joyously powerful that it might take their breath away. Even the Doctor, so used to so many different environments, was moved to shield his eyes and put a steadying hand upon his own chest. The children stumbled backwards. Ollus was literally open-mouthed in shock. Jenibeth started to cry without restraint, this physical catalyst seeming to release all her grief in one go. Sabel suddenly lost all self-control and threw herself at the Doctor's leg, hiding her face behind the pocket of his tweed jacket.

'It's going to be all right, it's going to be all right!' he shouted, trying to sound as reassuring as possible over the terrible din.

Finally, the open doors of the airlock clunked into place. Through the still dazzling brightness, the Doctor could make out the sound of heavy footsteps padding towards them, accompanied by the tight jangle of what was surely military equipment. Bobbing shadows of combat troops in helmets, brandishing formidable energy weapons, played over them.

Ollus and Jenibeth instantly ran to join their sister, clasping onto the Doctor. Ollus, clawing frantically, suddenly as determined as a scared kitten escaping up a curtain, scaled the Doctor's coat and put his hands around the Time Lord's neck. Jenibeth was close behind, settling on the Doctor at chest level.

The Doctor suddenly found himself in the role of some kind of pack horse, detailed to child-carrying duties, as the military squad encircled him, pointing their guns, scanning relentlessly for any sign of a hostile move.

'We're unarmed!' shouted the Doctor. 'No need to panic! These are children, not offensive weapons.'

A few moments later, the military team, without

a word and with no expressions visible behind their assault masks, were escorting the Doctor and his surrogate family across a precarious-looking gantry. It was now that it became clear what the strange, rumbling noise had been, distorted as it was through the metal layers of the ship's hull.

Several hundred feet below them, basking in a vibrant, glowing Carthedian sunset, was a vast crowd of people, numbering around ten thousand, the Doctor guessed. They stared up, waving flags and banners enthusiastically, roaring delightedly as every single one of them seemed to catch sight of the Doctor and the children at once.

The Doctor wondered what all this fuss was about; but he, Ollus, Jenibeth and Sabel were not allowed to dawdle and take in the sheer spectacle of their welcome. The soldiers pushed them on across the gantry and into a vast building in front of them. The Doctor suspected this might be some kind of 'border control' area.

As they cleared the entrance port, an iris-like door sealed behind them and, for a moment, it appeared as though they were in complete darkness. Blinking frantically, the Doctor realised they were in fact illuminated by a pale, greenish light. Suddenly, the soldiers plucked the children away from the Doctor. He tried to protest.

'Now, wait a minute! There's no need to be so—'

But he found himself brutally pushed back as the children were pulled away. Jenibeth cried loudly again, sobbing bitterly, her eyes darting around in confusion. The Doctor tried to catch her gaze, hoped he did, and mouthed 'It's all right' to her. It had no outward effect. Ollus and Sabel had fallen into a kind of numb, terrified silence. Along with the Doctor, they were all deposited into well-worn, padded chairs, spaced at equal intervals across this large, dark chamber. The chairs instantly locked them all into seated positions by way of mechanical grips, presumably activated remotely.

'It's all right, don't struggle,' said the Doctor, as the soldiers retreated into the darkness.

Within seconds, the Doctor found himself blinded again, this time by a pulsing, tingling light accompanied by a deep, electronic throbbing noise, almost like a heartbeat. As this sensory onslaught continued, he managed to pick out the shapes of the seated children next to him. They were undergoing the same process.

Decontamination, he thought. He wanted to say it aloud to reassure the children, but the sound was so loud, and there was something in this strange, pulsing beam that was stopping the muscles in his face from working.

Just when it seemed as though there would be no end to this browbeating, everything went silent. He realised he was exhausted, overheated, as if he had been running for his life. His eyelids weighing down over his eyes, he managed another glance at the children. They were now unconscious.

Then, a blast of freezing air shot out at them from all sides and above, billowing like frosty steam. Just as he began to shiver, the already dim light dialled down to total darkness and time seemed suspended.

*

With a gasp, the Doctor was awake again. Blazing lights *again*. This is getting tiresome, he thought. Bright, dark, hot, cold… what next?

'Are you aware that at 08.54 Carthedian standard time yesterday, a report was received from Captain J. L. Gafeska of the cargo ship *Axious* that the occupants of charter ship KS55NZ/4 were found dead aboard said charter ship?'

Ah, questions. They always came next. The voice was hard, efficient, trained to be emotionless, but it was definitely human. As the glare of the lights faded a little, the Doctor realised he was sitting opposite a uniformed woman, seated at a desk, tapping a small tablet-style computer. She glanced up at him, clearly impatient for an answer.

'I've got a question for you,' said the Doctor, not really able to manage a smile. 'Where are Sabel, Ollus and Jenibeth?'

'Answer the question, please,' said the woman, with an empty, insincere politeness.

'No,' said the Doctor.

'No, you won't answer the question?' she asked.

'No as in "no" is the answer to your question. Anyway, it's a stupid question, because obviously the children are alive. Whoever this Captain Gafeska is, he obviously didn't check very thoroughly, did he? Now, where are the children?'

The woman clearly had no intention of answering the Doctor's questions. For a moment, he thought he saw a trace of amusement twitch at her mouth, as if the very notion of her answering someone else's questions was ludicrous. She glanced back at her computer tablet and drew breath.

'Oh, next question,' interrupted the Doctor. The woman looked faintly annoyed. 'I wonder what that might be, hmm? How did I get aboard the ship? What's that funny blue crate thing? Who am I? Where do I come from? How come we don't have any records of you in our database? Am I getting close?'

The woman let her computer tablet fall to the desk with a clatter. She looked the Doctor straight in the eyes. The Doctor nodded. He knew this was a 'Look, I'm just doing my job' moment, and he was clearly not making it easy for her. She raised her eyebrows, almost, he thought, as if she were reading his mind.

'All right, all right,' he sighed. 'I'll try to be a bit more helpful. My name's the Doctor. The blue crate is my ship and yes, I know that's odd. I come from a long way away. I was just passing and picked up a distress call. I didn't get there in time, but the ship had been attacked by Daleks—'

'By Daleks?' the woman seemed genuinely shocked.

'Oh yes, of course,' said the Doctor. 'You think the Daleks are nice. Sabel told me. Well, you couldn't be more—'

'Nice?' interrupted the woman. 'The Dalek Foundation is responsible for—'

'The Sunlight Worlds, whatever they are, yeah, I know, Sabel told me that too. She's a bright kid. In fact, they're all bright kids. Very bright. What have you done to them? Are they all right?'

'They...' the woman stopped, realising, thought

the Doctor, that she had been tricked into answering someone else's question. She sighed. 'They're fine,' she said, smiling genuinely.

'Fine? I doubt that,' said the Doctor. 'They've just lost their parents.'

'Yes. Do you know how?'

'Haven't you looked at the flight log?' asked the Doctor.

The woman slowly shook her head. 'The datastore was blank.'

'Not when I saw it, it wasn't,' said the Doctor. 'Are you sure?'

The woman consulted her tablet. She shook her head again, then returned her gaze to the Doctor, leaning towards him a fraction. 'You're saying you saw something on the flight log?'

'Terrin and Alyst Blakely walked straight out of the airlock of that ship and killed themselves,' he said, bluntly.

'You actually saw that?' she asked.

The Doctor suddenly had an uncomfortable feeling that he knew where all this was going to end up. 'No,' he said. 'But I heard it and the flight log had a record of the airlock having been operated.'

'But—' the woman started.

'The datastore of the flight log is blank,' finished the Doctor. 'Yeah. So you probably think I'm lying. What do you think, then? I killed Terrin and Alyst and then... what? Brought their children home? I can't see that that makes much sense.'

The woman stared at him for a long time. The Doctor

could see she really did want to know the truth. Then she looked down at her tablet again. She was checking something.

'What's your name?' asked the Doctor.

Without looking up, she said, 'I'm not allowed to tell you my name.'

'Not very friendly,' said the Doctor, giving her his best boyish, charming smile. She did not look up to see it.

'I'm not your friend,' she said. His smile faded. And then she looked at him again.

He could see the very beginnings of a smile in her eyes, that twitch at the side of her mouth again; but once again, she suppressed it.

'What about my blue crate?' he asked.

'You can go now,' she said, simply.

Unceremoniously marched down a brightly lit corridor by another soldier in full face mask, the Doctor soon found himself reunited with the children. They were sitting on some rather battered-looking comfy chairs in a sort of waiting area. When the Doctor entered, they looked round in anticipation. It struck him that perhaps Ollus and Jenibeth were hoping against hope that, somehow, their parents had returned. For a split second, they looked as if they were about to launch themselves towards him in delight, but then they deflated, their eyes taking on a rather dull, haunted look.

Sabel just stared at the Doctor. He felt as if she was looking right into his thoughts; but then he realised that what he was thinking must have been fairly obvious from his expression. What in the world was he going to do with these children? Why was he being reunited with them anyway?

'We told them the truth,' Sabel said, simply.

The Doctor shrugged, trying to be cheerful. 'Always the best policy! So, how are we all, then?'

They didn't answer. It was, the Doctor realised, a bit of a stupid question.

'They thought you might have killed our parents,' continued Sabel. 'But we told them it was the Daleks.'

'And they didn't believe us, they didn't,' said Ollus.

'No,' said the Doctor. 'No, they didn't believe me either... Not enough evidence to prove anything. But we've got to find a way to *make* them believe us.'

'Why?' asked Jenibeth. 'What's the point?'

'Because... Well, because the Daleks are always up to no good,' said the Doctor. 'So these people here need to be warned, especially if they think the Daleks are...' he screwed his face up, '... nice.'

'How will you make everyone believe?' asked Ollus.

'I don't know,' admitted the Doctor. 'And what's more, I don't even know how I'm going to get the TARDIS back.'

At that moment, the door opened and the woman who had interrogated the Doctor breezed through, clearly not expecting to see them there.

'Oh,' she said, stopping.

'The girl with no name,' said the Doctor, smiling.

'What are you still doing here?' she asked, a little blankly.

'Um... Where are we supposed to go?' asked the

Doctor, gesturing around the room.

'The exit is through this door and down the corridor,' the woman explained.

'And that's it, is it?' asked the Doctor. 'I just leave here with three children and… where do we go? What do we do?'

'That's not our problem,' said the woman. 'There'll be a full examination of the ship. An investigation. If you're needed, we'll find you.'

'Oh, will you?' the Doctor smiled, intrigued.

'You've been implanted with a data-chip,' she said, as if he should have known.

'Oh. Nice. Thanks,' said the Doctor. 'Isn't that an infringement of my inalienable rights or something?'

'No,' she said, moving off towards another door on the other side of the room.

'That's it, then?' said the Doctor, starting to hurry after her.

She turned and looked at him, a little alarmed, he thought, as if she was considering calling for security or something.

'Yes, that's it,' she said, turning and exiting through the other door.

'Well,' said the Doctor, turning back to the children, his arms wide in one of his larger shrugs. Before he could say anything else, they had assembled in front of him in their customary formation again. He knew he was going to have to take all this one moment at a time.

As they headed down the corridor to the building's exit, the Doctor was trying to fathom how he was going to get back to the TARDIS, how he was going to convince the people of this world that the Daleks were a force for evil and, perhaps most importantly, how exactly he was going to look after three orphaned children without anywhere to live and with no money in his pocket.

When they passed through the main doors, the Doctor immediately saw a potential solution to one of those problems.

It was now night, but in the brightly illuminated street in front of them, there was a crowd of around a hundred people. Perhaps not as impressive as the thousands they had seen earlier, but, thought the Doctor, this gathering would do... especially since they had a very particular air about them.

Immediately, the crowd seemed to move almost as one, dashing towards the Doctor, Sabel, Ollus and Jenibeth. Dazzling lights from hand-held holo-cameras bobbed and swayed closer and closer. A gabble of overlapping questions started firing at them. These, the Doctor realised, were journalists.

'How did you find the ship? What happened to their parents? Who are you? What do you think of the reports that everyone on board had been killed? Did you know about the strength of public reaction back home?'

More and more questions piled on top of other questions and the more the Doctor and the children did not answer, the more versions of the same questions came firing at them in an increasingly grotesque symphony of intrusive craving. So far, the Doctor reflected, shutting off his mind from the dazzling lights and the incessant questioning, he had encountered two unpleasant aspects of human social behaviour on

Carthedia: uncaring officiousness and a rampantly insensitive press. Not rating as one of his favourite planets, that was for sure.

As he held up his hands in an attempt to stop the flood of questions, the Doctor realised that Sabel, Ollus and Jenibeth were all hiding inside his jacket. Ollus had actually fastened one of the buttons, so from just below the waist up, the Doctor now looked like a sort of bulging, tweed tent with a head.

'Please! Please! Please!' the Doctor shouted at the top of his voice. 'There are children here!'

But the journalists either simply did not care or did not hear.

The Doctor fished inside his jacket and pulled out his sonic screwdriver. He held it aloft, portentously. Some of the journalists looked up for a moment, but still their questions and grappling for position continued.

Flicking the sonic controls to a high oscillation, the Doctor activated the device and about twenty or so of the nearest street lamps exploded in a shower of dancing sparks. A nearby, oval-ish tram-like vehicle, very probably on its last night-time journey back to the depot, also bore the brunt of this sonic assault, as the metal pick-up arm on its roof sizzled furiously on the overhead cables, causing the whole tram to skitter off its tracks and into some parked, domed car-like vehicles.

Fortunately, the impacts were fairly minor, and no one was hurt.

All this commotion, however, was, thankfully, enough to stop the journalists long enough for the Doctor to get a word in. Realising that this might be his only chance, the Doctor knew he had to go for the big story first.

'The Daleks are evil!' he cried at the top of his voice. It had the desired effect. The journalists all looked at him. 'Well,' said the Doctor. 'That's better. You all look pretty gobsmacked. So, now then, *there's* a story for you, right there! I don't know how long you've been thinking the Daleks were your friends, but I'm here to tell you that you can be sure that they are up to something. I'm not sure what it is, but it has something to do with the planet Gethria. Some secret so terrible that the parents of these children were prepared to make the ultimate sacrifice to keep it from them. But let me tell you…'

For a moment he trailed off, noticing that the journalists were starting to peel away, shaking their heads. He heard words like 'nutter' and 'lunatic' and worse drift towards him. They were simply finding his story completely unacceptable.

The Doctor reached out and grabbed the arm of one of the retreating hacks, an older, grey haired, balding man in a heavy, dark coat.

'Wait a minute!' the Doctor pleaded. 'Why's all this so difficult for you to believe? I mean, you're journalists, aren't you? Don't you love a juicy bit of scandal? This could be a great story.'

'A great story?' the journalist sneered. He fixed the Doctor with a look. The Doctor looked straight back into his eyes. This was a veteran of the news trade, the Doctor could see that. A hardened man who felt he had seen it all. He had waited out here in the dark for several hours to get hold of a great story, and instead, all he had got was something totally crazy from a madman.

'You want us to say that the Daleks are evil?' he asked, dumbfounded.

'Why not?' asked the Doctor. 'It's true, and I can prove it to you!'

The journalist opened his arms wide, inviting the proof.

The Doctor found himself wrong-footed. 'Well, not now... obviously, but—'

'Look, the Daleks created the Sunlight Worlds,' the journalist explained.

Those Sunlight Worlds again, thought the Doctor. What *were* they?

The journalist was still talking. 'They've made life better for a generation of people whose lives were ruined by the worst galactic recession on record. You're going to have to do a lot better than shouting wild accusations in the street to get anyone to believe they're anything but... well, to be frank, saviours!'

'When did they create these... Sunlight Worlds?' asked the Doctor.

'Oooh, I dunno,' the journalist said. 'About thirty or forty years ago. Something like that. I've got an aunt who lives there. Says it's like paradise!'

'Paradise?' interrupted the Doctor, aghast. 'The Daleks created paradise?'

'Yeah!' said the journalist. 'So are you seriously telling me that makes the Daleks evil?'

To the Doctor's intense annoyance, he could find no answer to this. As the journalist retreated down the street, the Doctor gazed around in frustration. How could you prove something so obvious to people who had clearly had such a different, distorted experience of the Daleks? And then he noticed that the children had emerged from inside his jacket. They were the next problem he had to solve.

'What's going to happen now?' asked Sabel.

The Doctor held up a finger, as if he was about to tell them something significant. But when he looked for an idea, it was as if the cupboard was bare. He was well and truly stumped.

He turned back to look into the building they had just exited. He pushed at the door. It was locked securely. He looked at the windows. Heavy shutters were now down.

'I'm cold,' said Jenibeth.

'Me too,' said Ollus.

'And it's way past our bedtimes,' said Sabel, as if the Doctor should have known that.

The Doctor scanned the darkened street for inspiration. They seemed to be in what looked like a run-down area of a great city. A long, straight road stretched off far into the distance, towards the high, bright lights of what must be skyscrapers, he thought. Closer at hand, a few shabby, unlit buildings, possibly shops or cafes littered some untidy wasteland. This enormous spaceship landing terminal had perhaps been built away from the main, and possibly more affluent inhabited areas, as a safety precaution against crash landings.

The Doctor's impromptu exploding of nearby street lamps had almost certainly made this area a good deal darker than usual. Perhaps surprisingly, the minor tramcar crash had caused only the smallest of consternations. Luckily for the Doctor, no one had connected this incident with the man in the tweed suit and his three children. There had been only one, sleeping passenger on the tram, and she looked like she had not even been woken by the impact. The driver was climbing onto the tram roof, trying to check the power pick-up arm. None of the owners of the three empty smashed cars had emerged. Feeling rather guilty about it all, the Doctor hoped the cars had, perhaps, been abandoned.

He looked back at the children again. They stared back up at him. There was nothing for it, he would have to use his sonic screwdriver to break into the spaceship terminal and somehow find a way to get back to the TARDIS. Checking around to make sure that there was no one looking, the Doctor moved close to the terminal's main door. But just as he was about to press the control to operate his sonic screwdriver, a terrible noise swooped in from above. A noise like a rusty wheel scraping against a blackboard – ear-piercing and distinctly unpleasant.

There were green flashing lights too, playing all around, and these, coupled with the horrible din, seemed to transform this dark little backwater of a street into something resembling the opening moments of some horrifically bad-taste alien rock concert.

The children once again ran for shelter under the Doctor's jacket. The tram driver nearly fell off his tram roof. The Doctor clamped his hands over his ears, wincing. All of them looked up to see a large, metallic vehicle descending.

'Oh dear,' murmured the Doctor. He knew a police car when he saw one.

'Stay where you are! Do not move!' echoed a distorted voice, bouncing off every hard surface in the area.

The vehicle finally touched down and the grating siren croaked to a halt. The green lights were still flashing all over the place as the door opened and three people in green and black leathery uniforms with blunt-looking peaked caps and tinted visors stepped out, pointing what were clearly weapons at the Doctor and the children.

'I haven't done anything!' shouted the Doctor, putting his hands up. The children put their hands up too. The Doctor nodded towards the door of the space terminal. 'You can check for yourself. The door's still locked.'

The police officers stood perfectly still, as if they had not heard him.

The Doctor glanced at the tram. The driver was standing on the roof of it now, looking over, scratching his head.

'Oh, and I'm sorry about the tram!' said the Doctor. 'It was an accident. Sorry. Really, really sorry.'

The middle one of the police officers put his weapon into a side holster on his hip. He immediately produced a waxy-looking piece of paper from his pocket and held it up firmly, like an old-fashioned town crier. He started to read from the paper, through his visor, in a rapid, staccato manner that suggested he was just going through some motions he had gone through many times before.

'You-are-not-obliged-to-say-anything-but-you-are-hereby-warned-that-comments-you-have-made-in-a-place-of-public-assembly-have-been-deemed-offensive-to-the-Dalek-Foundation-and-as-such-are-classified-as-incitement-to-hatred-under-Carthedian-law—'

'Incitement to hatred? This is ridiculous!' said the Doctor. Then he thought to himself, I suppose I was trying to incite hatred of the Daleks. What's wrong with that?

'And-therefore-under-the-Prevention-of-Hatred-Act-9/70-3/4-you-are-hereby-to-be-taken-into-custody-and-detained-until-such-time-as-a-hearing-can-be-scheduled-for-you-to-justify-your-actions-and-words.'

'Custody?' the Doctor said. 'But what about…?' He was pointing to the children. Already, one of the other police officers was approaching the children, threateningly.

'You are no longer deemed a responsible guardian for these minors, and therefore, in accordance with Carthedian Child Protection laws, these children, namely Sabel Blakely, Jenibeth Blakely and Ollus Blakely are to be made wards of the state until such time as you are released from custody and once again deemed a fit guardian,' said the officer approaching the children.

'Fit guardian? *I'm* not a fit guardian!' protested the Doctor, as the police officer stepped swiftly forward, twisted the Doctor around and fitted his wrists with some form of handcuff.

'Doctor! Please!'

It was Sabel crying out as she, Ollus and Jenibeth were ushered firmly into the police vehicle. The Doctor realised that it was the first time any of the children had referred to him directly by name.

'You can't let them take us away!' said Sabel, her eyes full of angry tears.

And in that instant, the Doctor knew he must take care of them.

'No!' he cried out. 'Stop!'

For a moment, the police officers stopped, very probably out of shock.

The leading officer, now putting his waxy paper away, turned to the Doctor, tilted his head to one side and flicked up his visor.

'What?' said the officer. One word alone, but drenched in the sentiment of 'Don't waste my time'.

'You can't take these children away. They're my responsibility,' the Doctor found himself saying. He looked at the children and saw that all three of them were looking straight at him. In this moment, they had all suddenly decided they belonged together. It was as simple as that.

'Not any more,' the officer said, flicking his visor back down again. 'They're wards of the state. Take them away!'

Chapter Four
Prisoners of the State

Locked inside a small compartment at the rear of the police skimmer, the Doctor could hear the muffled sobs of Jenibeth. From what he could make out, Sabel was comforting her. He couldn't hear anything from Ollus, except the sporadic, strange little whizz and pop noises from his spaceship toy.

Through a narrow, smudged, metal-meshed window, the Doctor could catch only glimpses of Carthedia at night. It did indeed seem as though the city below was enormous. There were vast, rising plumes of steam or smoke, and as they drew nearer to what the Doctor assumed was the centre of the city, the lights below became more vibrant, and many more flying vehicles buzzed through the night air.

At one point, the vehicle landed and he heard the children being taken away. Sabel called out 'Doctor!' to him, only the second time she had called him that. The Doctor called back, trying to reassure her, but he was fairly certain she could not hear him. He hated the thought of them being put into some institution. From his brief encounters with Carthedian state hospitality so far, he didn't hold out much hope as to the warmth of compassion with which wards of the state might be treated here.

The police skimmer lifted off again, leaving the children far behind, travelling further and further across the city, occasionally sounding its screeching siren, to get other vehicles to fly out of the way, the Doctor assumed. Finally, the skimmer descended into a large, dark chamber. The Doctor heard something enormous and metallic crashing shut above them. He imagined they had made a vertical landing inside into some kind of police station.

The door to his tiny cell was suddenly wrenched open and he was roughly manhandled out of the vehicle, his limbs aching from being so cramped.

'Where now, then?' asked the Doctor of the green and black police officers. None of them had anything to say to him. He could see their tired eyes through their visors. This was probably the end of their night shift, thought the Doctor. They were clearly not in the mood for idle conversation with prisoners accused of hate crimes.

They took him across a large, aerodrome-like space, where other similar police vehicles were parked. From there into an elevator, through several dimly lit corridors filled with unpleasant smells, muted chatter and howls of protest, pain and anguish from cells and custody suites... and finally into a strangely incongruous, wood-panelled room.

Here, all was quiet. All three police officers left him alone, the door sucking shut behind them, sealing out the noise of the police station.

The Doctor waited, sitting on a padded bench, breathing in the sweet, varnished air. He was pretty certain this was some kind of courtroom. Ahead of him was a raised platform with an elaborately sculpted, grand wooden desk built into it. There were two other, smaller desks to the left and right of it.

Moments passed. The Doctor's mind was racing. He had the distinct suspicion that he was about to be swallowed up by the petty, legal complexities of this human colony planet. He knew he was going to have to extract himself from all this pretty soon if he was going to have any chance of finding out what the Daleks were up to and how to stop them.

An almost invisibly fitted wooden door swung open behind the large desk and a man in a plain black suit with a high-collared black shirt and a thin silver metal strip on his lapel entered without looking at the Doctor and sat down at the desk. From the light suddenly illuminating the man's face, the Doctor assumed there was some kind of computer screen built into the wooden surface. This must be the judge, he thought to himself.

The judge glanced at each of the desks to his left and right, expectantly. A faint sense of disapproval passed over his small, flattish, pale face.

The Doctor tutted out loud. The judge immediately fixed him with his surprisingly beady eyes. The Doctor attempted an affable smile.

'Late, are they?' he ventured, tutting again.

The directness of the judge's stare faded as he looked back down at his desk computer screen, apparently losing interest in the Doctor.

Another hidden door swung open behind the right-hand desk, and another man in a black suit, this time with a green metallic strip on his lapel, came dashing in, holding a sheaf of waxy papers. His red hair was ruffled and he looked like he had cut himself shaving. There was a somewhat panicked air about him. He nodded respectfully to the judge and rushed over to the Doctor. Without looking at the Doctor's face, he held out a hand. The Doctor shook it, watching this new arrival shuffle through the papers.

'Dansard, Hellic Dansard,' he said. 'State-appointed defence council.'

'Got you up in the middle of the night, did they?' asked the Doctor, with a smile. Hellic stopped for a moment and looked at the Doctor properly for the first time.

'Er... something like that,' he said. 'You seem pretty cheerful for a man in a lot of trouble.'

'Oh, I'm always in a lot of trouble,' said the Doctor, his smile getting bigger.

'Riiight,' said Hellic, clearly not sure what to make of the Doctor. 'The evidence seems pretty irrefutable. Several of the press submitted footage of you saying the Daleks are evil. Can't really see any way around that.'

'Neither can I,' said the Doctor. 'The Daleks *are* evil.'

'Ah... yeah,' said Hellic, his voice becoming more hushed. 'Probably not a good idea to keep saying things like that.'

At that moment, another hidden door swung open, this time behind the left-hand desk. The Doctor was expecting to see another black-suited lawyer. But instead, he was confronted with...

A Dalek.

Bronze, squat, smoothly scraping the wooden surface of the door, manoeuvring expertly into the tiny space behind the desk, this Dalek was clearly the prosecuting council. The judge looked up, giving a brief but reverential nod to the Dalek. Hellic nodded too, then returned his gaze to the Doctor, clearly intending to continue their briefing.

The Doctor was completely taken aback by the Dalek's entrance. He knew that these people here on Carthedia had been fooled into thinking the Daleks were some kind of force for good, but he still had not expected to find Daleks acting as public servants in legal cases.

'Dalek Litigator,' said the judge in a spiky little voice, allowing himself a smile – a rather smug smile, thought the Doctor. 'We do not often have the honour of your presence in the police courts.'

Dalek Litigator? That was a new one, thought the Doctor. He studied the Dalek, which did not reply to the judge's rather oily welcome. Nothing extraordinary about this specimen, thought the Doctor. Just a standard, bronze Dalek. But then... there was...

Something.

The Doctor blinked, feeling slightly woozy. He felt himself falling forwards for a moment. He found himself steadied by Hellic.

'Are you all right?' asked Hellic.

'Um…' the Doctor managed to say, feeling a distinct sense of nausea. He looked up at the Dalek Litigator again. For a moment, its entire form seemed to blur. The Doctor shook his head and blinked again. The blur shrank to the grating section below the Dalek's dome, then cork-screwed away altogether, like misty water swirling down a plughole.

'Doctor?' asked Hellic.

'What?' asked the Doctor, snapping back to reality. 'What's going on here?'

'The file says that is what you're known as,' said Hellic.

'Oh… er… yes…' said the Doctor, still disorientated.

'Look, I wanted to ask you about the children,' said Hellic.

'The children… yes, Sabel, Ollus and Jenibeth…' said the Doctor, suddenly feeling some urgency, remembering the muted sound of Jenibeth's sobbing. 'What's happened to them? I must find out what's—'

'All right, all right,' said Hellic, glancing over his shoulder. 'I'll try something on that front. Hold tight. Here we go.'

Hellic nodded to the judge. The judge touched something on his desk and an electronic chiming sound rang out three times.

'Court now in session,' said the judge.

The Dalek's eyestalk raised and fixed its blue glare on the Doctor. The Doctor stared right back at it.

The judge began to read the charge. 'You are charged with incitement to hatred. The specifics are that you made unsubstantiated claims in a public place as to the morality and public standing of the Dalek Foundation…'

The Doctor drew breath to speak, but stopped when he heard a hissing noise from Hellic.

'Not yet,' mouthed Hellic at him, shaking his head.

'Dalek Litigator,' continued the judge. 'This is a criminal matter, as the state of Carthedia deplores all hate crimes. Do you wish to apply for punitive damages against the accused?'

The Dalek's voice cut through the courtroom like a chainsaw through soft wood. 'Maximum punitive damages. All assets to be seized,' it said, still fixing its glare upon the Doctor.

How could anyone on this planet think something that spoke like *that* was a force for good? thought the Doctor. This was insane.

'Very well,' continued the judge, calmly, for all the world as if he had just been speaking to his maiden aunt. 'Your claim is so entered. How does the accused plead?'

'Guilty,' said the Doctor.

Hellic clapped a hand to his unruly hair. He jerked his head forward and glared at the Doctor as if to say 'You idiot'.

'What?' asked the Doctor. 'I am. I am guilty of saying the Daleks are evil, because THEY ARE!' he suddenly shouted, rising to his feet.

Instinctively, the Doctor flinched, suddenly expecting his rash outburst to be met with a cry of 'Exterminate!' from the Dalek Litigator. He imagined that he would have to crash to the floor to avoid the burst of energy screaming from the Dalek's gun. Its full power would burst into the wall, blowing a huge hole in it, through which the Doctor could escape in all the confusion, following the route back to the aerodrome, which he'd carefully memorised, then getting in a police skimmer which he would crash through the roof. Somehow he would find the children and *somehow* he would find the TARDIS and work out a way to turn this mad, upside down world up the right way again…

But none of that happened. There was merely silence. Hellic looked down and shuffled his papers in despair. The judge looked faintly irritated, gently expelling a controlled sigh and letting his eyelids blink slowly.

'Well then…' the judge finally said, tapping at his computer. 'Your plea is so entered.'

'Er…' started Hellic.

The judge, the Dalek Litigator and the Doctor all turned to him. What kind of extraordinary lawyer was this? wondered the Doctor. His client had just rashly confessed to being guilty, but this lawyer was still going to give something a go. The Doctor couldn't help but smile, broadly, in unabashed admiration.

'Um, there's the issue of the children,' offered Hellic. 'Testimony from the arresting officers clearly shows there is a degree of emotional attachment—'

'Emotional attachment to a man who incites hatred in the streets?' scoffed the judge.

'Emotional attachment to a man who saved their lives,' offered Hellic, almost apologetically.

'There is no recorded evidence of the Doctor rescuing the children,' the Dalek suddenly croaked, bluntly.

'But there is no recorded evidence that says he *didn't* rescue them,' countered Hellic. 'And he did arrive on Carthedia with them *and* they clearly wanted to stay with him when he was apprehended – the officers will testify to that.'

Again, the Doctor half-expected the Dalek to deal with this with a blast of searing energy, suspending Hellic in an excruciating halo of blinding, negative light. But the Dalek merely glared at Hellic, then returned its gaze to the Doctor.

'What are you proposing?' asked the judge.

'That the Doctor should be able to visit the children on compassionate grounds before sentence is passed,' said Hellic.

'Oh, you're good,' said the Doctor.

'Silence!' asserted the judge, almost as sharply as a Dalek might.

Hellic did not seem happy at the Doctor's interjection. He shook his head admonishingly at the Doctor.

The judge sighed again and then turned to the Dalek Litigator.

'I can only grant such access if there is no objection from the prosecution,' said the judge.

That was the end of that, then, thought the Doctor. He watched the Dalek as its eyestalk twitched and swayed slightly. It looked from the judge to the Doctor, to Hellic and then back to the Doctor.

'No objection,' it said.

Chapter Five
The Orphanage

The Doctor found himself once again sitting inside a police skimmer, his mind still reeling from the shock that the Dalek Litigator had not objected to his visiting the children. That had been... odd. What were the Daleks up to? First they hadn't destroyed the Blakelys' ship, and now this.

This time, he was not in the cramped, secure cell at the rear of the skimmer, but sitting on the back seat with his state-appointed lawyer, Hellic Dansard.

Vibrating and shuddering, the skimmer was lifting off towards the roof of the aerodrome building where the Doctor had landed a few hours before. This time, with bigger windows to look out of, he got a clear view of the aerodrome's great ceiling opening. There was early morning light in the sky outside and, as they shot past the now closing roof, the Doctor could see more of the detail of the city. It appeared to be a vast collection of prefabricated pods and containers, all of varying ages, apparently erected and welded onto each other over the years, so that the city had the strange appearance of a collection of odd, brutal shapes that had somehow grown all over each other like a bizarre, metallic fungus.

The Doctor turned to Hellic and smiled. Hellic was fatigued, nodding off.

'They really did get you out of bed, didn't they?' said the Doctor, smiling.

Hellic jolted back into his seat, suddenly awoken by the Doctor's words. He frowned, irritated at the disturbance.

'Thanks for what you did,' said the Doctor.

'I did my job,' said Hellic, groggily.

'You needn't have done,' said the Doctor. 'Especially since I pleaded guilty.'

'I was just being professional,' Hellic said simply. 'Don't confuse that with compassion.'

There was that Carthedian charm again... or rather, the lack of it.

'And you people really think this Dalek Foundation is a force for good, do you?' asked the Doctor.

'Of course,' said Hellic.

'So... You really do think I'm some kind of Dalek-hating nutcase, then?'

'Yes.'

The Doctor leaned close to him. 'So why did you get me visitation rights to the children?'

'Because you were entitled to them,' said Hellic. 'And there was clear evidence of an emotional attachment, which the police officers noted in their statements.'

The Doctor nodded. 'Fair enough. You're a professional. Well done, you.'

Hellic turned and looked at the Doctor, resigned to being awake now. 'Why did you say what you did about the Daleks, when you knew they would prosecute?'

'Prosecute?' chuckled the Doctor. 'I'm lucky the Daleks didn't exterminate me. But seriously, Hellic, tell me, what would you say if I told you I'd seen the Daleks carrying out the most appalling acts of war? That I've witnessed countless atrocities committed by them and seen the results of their terrifying deeds in the burial pits of a thousand worlds?'

Hellic's eyes did not flinch as he studied the Doctor, considering. 'I'd say...' he started, then stopped. 'Are you serious?'

'I'm serious,' said the Doctor.

'I'd say, show me some proof,' said Hellic.

But the Doctor knew he had none to hand.

Jenibeth had probably not stopped sobbing all night, Sabel realised as she awoke in the unfamiliar blankets of the dank, hard bed they were sharing. Several hours ago, she had got used to her sister's crying and had nodded off, but now it was the hard rain rattling against the tall windows of this draughty room that had awoken her. And poor Jeni was still crying in a squeaky, hoarse little voice.

Sabel leant over to her and smoothed her hair.

'Crying won't do any good, Jeni,' she whispered as kindly as she could.

'I can't help it,' Jeni croaked back.

Sabel could see Ollus in the bed next to them. He was fast asleep, clutching his spaceship.

Jeni's sobs were getting quieter now. Probably only because she was tired out, thought Sabel. She smoothed her sister's hair again and asked her if she had any jelly blobs left.

Jeni shook her head. So Sabel told her to think about jelly blobs and imagine she was eating a delicious, red one.

'Imagine the juiciness in your mouth, think about how lovely it would be,' said Sabel.

Jeni started chewing a pretend jelly blob and gave a little smile.

Sabel looked around their room. It was small and narrow, but with a very high ceiling. There were damp, rusty patches on the faded, light blue walls and the floor was covered in stains and smudged footprints. There was a musty sort of smell and rain was dripping through cracks in the frames of the tall, thin windows.

She thought about Mummy and Daddy and felt a deep ache in her chest that seemed to squeeze the breath out of her. She would not cry, though. She had told Jeni it would do no good, so she *would not* cry.

'Will the funny Doctor man come back?'

Sabel realised Ollus was suddenly wide awake and talking to her, looking over to her from his bed, still hugging his spaceship.

'I think he's gone,' said Sabel. 'I don't think he's coming back.'

'I thought he was going to look after us,' said Ollus.

Pausing to stop chewing her pretend jelly blob, Jenibeth said, 'He's gone away like Mummy and Daddy.'

'No,' said Sabel. 'Mummy and Daddy are dead. The Doctor isn't dead.'

'How do you know?' asked Ollus. 'I expect those policemen killed him.'

Just then, there was a loud rumbling sound from outside the windows. Sabel jumped out of bed and ran to the nearest window. There, through the smudged and dirty, plastic glass, she could just about see a big, green and black skimmer landing. It bumped down onto the hard, wet surface of the area outside. Then, the doors opened and some people got out. There were two policemen, a man in a black suit and...

Sabel's heart felt like it was bumping up and down for a moment. And that confused her. Why was she feeling like this? She tried to speak, but she couldn't. It was as if the words had got clogged up in her throat, and she felt that if she forced them out, she would cry and cry just like her sister. And she was afraid that she might never stop.

Ollus jumped out of bed and ran to her side. He looked out of the window and said what Sabel could not.

'It's the funny Doctor man!'

He was coming back. This strange man who had given them the worst news they had ever heard... He was coming back to rescue them.

In that instant, it became clear to Sabel how much she had given up on any hope. She had felt empty, filled with a hurt that ran deeper than she had ever imagined hurt could go. But now, this man who she had not even liked, was coming back. And even though she had hated him for the bad news he had given them, for some reason she could not really work out, Sabel felt sure that this strange, funny man in his funny clothes, with his big, smiley face and his glowing, buzzing screwdriver that made lights explode... She felt that he was the answer to everything.

The Doctor walked across the wet courtyard towards what Hellic had told him was the Carthedia State Orphanage. Even though, like the rest of the city, it was made from a collection of intricately welded together containers and pods, the Doctor could not shake the feeling that there was something distinctly Victorian and imposing about it. Against the thundery sky and lashing rain, it looked like it had emerged straight from a ghost story. A ghost story where young orphans were kidnapped and locked up in a scary mansion.

The police officers were keeping a wary but weary eye on the Doctor. It was probably long past time for them to clock off. Hellic indicated a large, metal doorway. It was caked in rust. As he tapped in an entrance code, it creaked unpleasantly open.

As they entered the building, walking down a long, echoing corridor towards a distant reception desk on a raised plinth at the end, Hellic moved closer to the Doctor.

'You'll only have about ten minutes with them,' he said, blankly.

'Today?' asked the Doctor.

'No, that'll be it,' said Hellic. 'Once sentence has been passed, all your guardian rights will be revoked and you'll be incarcerated.'

'Oh, you're all heart on this planet, aren't you?' said the Doctor. 'And when will sentence be passed?'

'It's probably happening right now, back in the courtroom.'

'Great,' said the Doctor, not meaning it at all. 'So you bringing me here is just sort of scoring professional points, isn't it? Building up your CV for a more senior post?'

Hellic ignored this and turned his attention to the reception desk they were now rapidly approaching. He pulled out another of his pieces of waxy paper from his inside jacket pocket and handed it to the rather squat, bald, bespectacled receptionist.

'Court order 5/679-4 relating to the Blakely children,' said Hellic.

'Oh yes,' mumbled the receptionist, typing something onto a flat screen on his desk. 'I remember them. One of them cried all night. Most annoying. Will they be staying long?'

'Probably until they come of age,' said Hellic.

'Hang on,' said the Doctor. 'Surely Terrin and Alyst left some provision for them in their will.'

Hellic turned to the Doctor, with a rather pitying look on his face. Pitying, but distinctly unsympathetic.

'You heard the Dalek Litigator. Maximum punitive damages. Total seizure of assets,' he said.

'I haven't got any assets,' said the Doctor. 'Well, apart from the TARDIS – oh, I see, you've seized that, have you? Of course you have. The Daleks would love to get their hands on the TARDIS.'

Hellic sighed. 'When I get the call through from the courtroom, you will be confirmed as a hate criminal. Your visiting rights will be revoked and all assets connected with the case will be seized by the Dalek Foundation.'

'You mean…' the Doctor felt naive for not anticipating the full heartlessness of the State of Carthedia. 'They're seizing the Blakelys' financial estate as well?'

'Of course,' said Hellic. 'And when questioned, the children did not denounce you.'

'Denounce? But… I was just honest about the Daleks,' said the Doctor.

'I'd advise you not to compound your crime. If you make your assertion about the Daleks again, I will be forced to report it and your sentence will most likely be increased,' said Hellic, as if this were all just a matter of course.

'Great defence council you turned out to be,' said the Doctor. 'Right. Where are the children? I want to see them now!'

Having been given instructions on how to find the room where the children were being kept, the Doctor quickened his pace, with Hellic scuttling after him to catch up. The two policemen did not hurry, but they were certainly making sure the Doctor was in range at all times.

As he walked along, the Doctor's mind was working overtime. He looked all around him. The metal walls, the rust everywhere. Paint peeling. Water dripping down. And this was where those poor children were expected to live until they were... what? Sixteen? Or older? He couldn't stand for that. But what could he do to get them and himself out of this hybrid futuristic-Dickensian nightmare?

The Doctor was thankful that a combination of fatigued officers and possibly inferior scanning technology had meant he still had his sonic screwdriver with him. Surreptitiously fiddling with its controls in his pocket, the Doctor was trying to fathom a way of using the rusting metal structure of the building to his advantage. But even if they were able to escape, where would they go?

One problem at a time, he decided. Get away first. Find a way back to the TARDIS later.

The tall door to a narrow little room was unlocked and opened in front of him. It revealed the pathetic sight of Sabel, Jenibeth and Ollus huddled on a bed, wrapped in a blanket, seemingly fearing the worst. The Doctor wasn't sure what kind of reception he'd get. They had been rather distrustful of him, but when they had been taken away, their appeals to him had told a different story.

Sabel leapt forward, dragging her brother and sister with her. 'We knew you'd come back!' she said joyously.

Jenibeth and Ollus let out little uncontrolled yelps of delight.

'Did you?' said the Doctor, smiling and rushing to them.

'Well... no,' said Ollus, bluntly. 'We thought the policemen might have killed you.'

'But we are glad to see you!' said Jenibeth, throwing

herself around the Doctor's neck, sobbing with delight.

This was heartbreaking for the Doctor. By being here, he had raised the children's hopes, but he knew he now probably had less than ten minutes with them before they would be locked away in this ghastly orphanage for the foreseeable future – and *he* was about to be imprisoned for hate crimes against the Daleks.

He realised he must act straight away. Hoping he had selected the right level of sonic vibration, he hastily whispered to the children.

'Put your fingers in your ears,' he hissed. Astonishingly, the children instantly obeyed him. Bright kids, he thought.

He flicked on the sonic screwdriver. The noise emitted was just about the most piercing sound he had ever managed to produce with the device, and the frequency at which it was bouncing off the metal walls of the room produced a vibration far in excess of the Doctor's expectations. The policemen instantly started gasping in pain, putting their hands to their ears. The shock actually knocked Hellic unconscious. He just crumpled as if his entire body had been made of the waxy paper he had stuffed in his pockets.

Then the Doctor focused the vibration on one of the outer walls with a window in it. Firstly, the glass shattered and the window frames fell out. Then, the ancient, rusted welding which held the walls together ruptured and three walls simply toppled outwards, leaving a whole section of the building exposed to the elements.

There, before them in the rain-pelted courtyard, was

the police skimmer.

'Run!' cried the Doctor.

As he launched himself across the bed, Jenibeth gripped the Doctor's neck tightly, clamping on to his chest by wrapping her legs around him. Ollus had seized a lapel and was holding on as hard as he could. Sabel started running and grabbed hold of the hand the Doctor shot out for her.

Staggering and flailing, they reached the skimmer and the Doctor tried the doors. Locked.

Sabel shouted, 'Oh no!'

'Don't worry,' smiled the Doctor, adjusting his sonic screwdriver.

'Is that your magic wand?' asked Ollus.

'Er… Sort of. Not always,' said the Doctor. And with a more controlled, buzzing vibration, it easily opened the skimmer door… Which was just as well.

From behind them, the voices of the policemen rang out. They had just recovered from their sonic ear-bashing.

'Stop! Stay where you are, or we fire!' they were shouting.

The Doctor was already entering the skimmer, throwing Jenibeth and Ollus over the front seats into the back and swinging Sabel into the front passenger seat, when he glanced back to see the policemen taking aim. He slammed the door shut behind them as shots rang out. Chunks of the courtyard exploded on impact and slammed against the skimmer doors.

The Doctor looked at the controls on the dashboard in front of him.

'Right!' he said, rubbing his hands together. 'How difficult can this be?'

'Quick!' shouted Sabel. The Doctor saw she had noticed the policemen running full pelt towards them. He quickly flipped a few controls. Power throbbed through the chassis of the skimmer.

'Good start!' the Doctor proclaimed, beaming.

'Hurry up!' squealed Jenibeth in a voice so high that for a moment the Doctor thought he had accidentally switched his sonic screwdriver back to maximum.

Suddenly, the policeman impacted with the skimmer, both of them grabbing at the doors with their hands.

'Um...' declared the Doctor, and quickly located another switch on the dashboard. There was a deep 'thunk-thunk' noise. 'Central locking!'

The policemen hammered on the doors in frustration. Then one of them stepped back and plunged a hand into his leathery pocket.

The Doctor, meanwhile, was still, rapidly poring over the other controls. Nothing was labelled very helpfully. He grunted in frustration.

Sabel started tugging at his arm and shouting, 'Come on-come on-come on!' Her brother and sister joined in.

'All right-all right-all right!' the Doctor shouted back at them. 'Don't rush me.'

Then... 'thunk-thunk', the central locking had been unlocked by the policemen.

The children looked at the Doctor in horror. He gave them an 'oh dear' look, then backed it up by actually saying, 'Oh dear.'

Through the windows, they could see the policemen

smiling, suddenly taking their time about everything, smug in their victory. One of them slowly aimed his gun, the other beckoned with a wiggling finger for them all to exit the skimmer. The Doctor could see Hellic staggering up behind them, having recovered from his sonic-induced fainting. He did not look pleased.

The Doctor and the children sat tight, almost as if they were pretending the policemen were not there.

'What are we going to do?' asked Ollus, not daring to look out of the windows.

'Sssh,' said the Doctor. 'I'm thinking.'

He heard the click of the door mechanism start to open. One of the policemen had lost patience and was coming in.

'I... think it's this one,' said the Doctor, his finger hovering over a button on the dashboard.

'What's this one?' asked Sabel.

'At least... I'm pretty sure,' said the Doctor. And he pressed it.

He and the children jerked back violently as the skimmer shot straight up into the sky, a perfect, emergency, vertical lift-off as if it had been propelled upwards by a massive, hidden spring underneath it.

'Geronimooooooo!' hollered the Doctor, his voice bumping and vibrating as the skimmer engines surged at full power. When he stopped hollering and decided to look at the dashboard controls again, the children were, he discovered, still screaming.

Chapter Six
On the Run

The policeman who had started to open the door of the skimmer had been thrown clear by the vehicle's sudden upward exit. He was lying on his back, groaning.

His comrade finished staring up at the rapidly diminishing shape of the skimmer in the sky and made what seemed like a reluctant attempt to pull the other policeman to his feet.

Hellic Dansard could not quite believe what he had witnessed. He had thought that his pedantic assigning of child visitation rights to this strange Doctor man would win him favour with the court judge. But now that this astute bit of legal manoeuvring had ended in his client escaping, the prospects for his future career were looking distinctly poor.

'How could you let them get away?' he asked the policemen, venting his frustration.

Both policemen were now standing. They both gave a look to Hellic that said, 'Don't push it, mate,' and then one of them spoke into a lapel transmitter.

'We need back-up,' he said. 'And fast.'

Meanwhile, the skimmer was still heading upwards. The Doctor had already noticed from the tone of the engine that the systems were straining to continue climbing. The thinness and cooling temperature of the air meant that they were very probably reaching the point of no return. Or rather, fast return – streaking back down to the surface of Carthedia with nothing to stop them but wishful thinking.

If only he could work out how to switch off the ascent thrusters and just drive this thing sensibly. He tried a few more controls, but they only made the interior lights come on and off and the windscreen wipers work.

Then a little voice came from behind his left ear.

'Shall I drive?'

It was Ollus. The Doctor smiled, determined not to scare the little boy by saying something like, 'Don't be stupid, you're only 4 years old!'

Then he caught Sabel's eye. She nodded enthusiastically.

'What? Seriously?' the Doctor mouthed to her.

'Daddy used to let him drive our skimmer all the time. Ever since he was two and a half,' she whispered in reply.

This little Ollus fellow was a living marvel, the Doctor decided – either that or they were all going to die horribly; and given that they were all about to die horribly anyway, he might as well take a risk on a little marvel of a 4-year-old. So, without pausing, he pulled Ollus over into the front seat, onto his lap.

'You're in command!' said the Doctor.

Ollus gave a confident little smile, popping his spaceship into his pocket. He then leaned forward, flicked a few switches and a semi-circular steering wheel unfolded from a hidden compartment in front of him.

'Oh, that's where it was,' said the Doctor.

A few more adjustments and Ollus had arrested their ascent. Grasping the wheel, the little boy effortlessly steered them down several thousand, breath-restoring feet. The temperature in the skimmer immediately rose to a more comfortable level and the air thickened up with oxygen.

'You're good!' said the Doctor, patting Ollus on the back heartily, before remembering he was only a little boy and should perhaps not be patted quite so heartily. Ollus gave a little surprised cough, but smiled nevertheless.

'I don't suppose you could find the spaceport, could you?' asked the Doctor.

Without speaking, Ollus tapped another control and a heads-up-display depicting a map of the city appeared on the windscreen. The Doctor started scrolling it by brushing his fingers over it. Fairly quickly, he located a large red square on the screen, labelled 'Spaceport'. Ollus leaned forward and pressed his finger firmly on this red square.

A muffled, disjointed, electronic voice burbled up from somewhere behind the dashboard. 'Location selected. Carthedia City Spaceport Terminal. Auto-pilot engaged.'

'An intelligent, onboard computer system!' cheered the Doctor, then leaned over to Sabel as if confiding something vastly important. 'Now *that* could come in handy.'

Meanwhile, the court judge who had presided over the Doctor's hate-crime case had just finished speaking to Hellic Dansard on a comms-link. He smacked his hand down on his office desk in frustration and stared angrily out of the window at the jagged skyline of the city.

'Idiot,' he murmured with restrained rage, through his teeth.

'It was to be expected,' came the harsh, grating voice of the Dalek Litigator, who had been present throughout the communication with the unfortunate Hellic.

'What do you mean?' asked the judge, surprised.

'The Doctor is known to the Daleks,' said the Litigator, flatly.

'Known? What do you *mean*?' asked the judge.

'He is a known saboteur of Dalek Foundation operations,' said the Dalek.

'Saboteur?' The judge was a little taken aback. 'If you have proof of other crimes he has committed, why didn't you mention these during the—'

'It is a matter to be dealt with by Dalek Foundation security forces,' the Dalek said, whirring and moving towards the judge menacingly.

For a moment, the judge felt an icy tinge of threat from the Dalek. He lifted his chin defensively, his eyes blinking into the burning, cold blue light of the Dalek's single eye.

'On this planet, all security matters are dealt with by our own police—' began the judge.

'Dalek security forces have been deployed at the spaceport terminal,' interrupted the Dalek. Its tone was relentless and to his surprise, the judge found that he dared not try to continue speaking. 'The embarkation zone where the Doctor's TARDIS is being held is now legally classified as Dalek sovereign territory.'

The judge felt almost as though the words of the Dalek were sucking his breath away, such was their sheer force. The electronic distortion was still ringing in his ears as he steeled himself to speak again. 'How can you be sure that's where this Doctor will—'

The Dalek's voice cut straight through the judge's words again. And what it said carried with it a deep hatred and knowledge that went far beyond the simplicity of this single, short, staccato sentence.

'We know the Doctor.'

The police skimmer was swooping down towards the spaceport terminal, when Jenibeth squealed, pointing out of the window.

Sabel, Ollus and the Doctor looked over to see what she was pointing at. The Doctor could see the spaceport ahead. It was a view of it he had not seen before. Behind the building in which he had been questioned were a series of massive, rectangular landing pads. Some contained ships, others featured enormous landing struts like the ones they had made their touchdown on the previous day. In fact, the Doctor could clearly see the ship the Blakely family had chartered, still supported in its landing position. But it wasn't the ships Jenibeth was squealing about…

On one of the main walkways between the many landing pads, something was moving. From above, for a moment, it looked rather like a strange, metallic centipede, weaving its way along. But on closer examination, the Doctor could see that each circular segment of this 'creature' bristled with two flashing lights and a single, twitching stalk. This was a large squad of Daleks, moving with purpose.

'Daleks,' muttered the Doctor. 'Like they're expecting me. Hmm. They're always expecting me. So they should.'

He turned to Ollus, who was playing with his spaceship toy again, ducking and diving it through the fizzing holograms it projected.

'Get ready to take us in on manual control,' said the Doctor.

Ollus immediately put his toy away into his pocket and returned his attention to the skimmer's controls.

'What if they see us?' asked Sabel. 'The Daleks, I mean.'

'I don't know,' mused the Doctor. 'I just don't know. You see, they're obviously trying to maintain the illusion of being…' he screwed up his face as he had done before at the thought of it, "*nice*". So they can't just start shooting at us.'

'Hey, there's something else!' called out Jenibeth. The Doctor and Sabel followed her gaze.

'Isn't that your crate thing that you said you arrived in?' asked Sabel.

'The TARDIS... yes,' said the Doctor, crestfallen. 'And it's parked right next to a Dalek ship.'

Sure enough, the TARDIS was on one of the landing pads. Most of the pad was taken up by the large, circular shape of a Dalek saucer; but next to it, just squeezed into a corner of the pad was the TARDIS. And there was a Dalek on guard at its door.

'Oh, this is just getting better and better,' said the Doctor, with a flicker of delight growing inside him. 'It's a really obvious trap.' It was one of those moments when he felt most alive. Pitted against an implacable enemy, he could almost *feel* his neurons firing.

'Are we going to run away?' asked Jenibeth.

'I definitely think we should run away,' said Sabel. 'Ollus, turn this thing around and—'

'No,' said the Doctor, giving the Blakely children a broad smile and a wink. 'I've got a plan.'

'What plan?' asked Sabel, looking terrified.

'Ollus,' the Doctor said. 'Hand me your spaceship.'

Hellic Dansard had clambered aboard another police skimmer, which the police had summoned to the orphanage. It was his plan to be instrumental in recapturing the Doctor. Not exactly a traditional role for a defence lawyer, but frankly he was prepared to do anything to win back favour with the police court judge.

As the skimmer rose high above the city, Hellic bobbed up and down to see if there was any sign of the escaping Doctor.

'Sit still, will ya?' one of the policemen snapped. 'You're rockin' the boat!'

'Any sign of them?' persisted Hellic. Then he looked over his shoulder as he heard several, deep whooshing sounds from behind. Out of the rear windows, he could see about ten other police skimmers approaching.

'Now that's what I call back-up,' said the other policeman.

'Squad Leader to all skimmers,' squawked a throaty voice from the comms-link speaker. 'Fugitive skimmer has been located approaching the main spaceport terminal. We are to proceed to intercept immediately. Let's get moving!'

Hellic hung on to his seat as his stomach seemed to rise unpleasantly towards his throat. He looked around him. All the skimmers, including the one he was in, were peeling off and heading downwards, as if to attack. He didn't know whether to feel excited or sick.

The Dalek guarding the TARDIS was scanning around the immediate vicinity. It had received command signals instructing it to prevent anyone from entering this craft at all costs. It knew that there was a whole squad of Daleks patrolling the area. If it came under attack, assistance would be close by.

Suddenly, for just a fraction of a second, its audio perceptors detected a noise from above. It recognised the sound as that of a Carthedian police skimmer. The Dalek scanned upwards. Nothing. Just the grey sky, rain falling and sporadic, distant skimmer traffic. This caused a disconnect in the Dalek's reasoning. If it sounded as if a Carthedian police skimmer was there, then why was it not there?

As it was about to transmit a report to its command unit, its perceptors were bombarded with an excess of unexpected information. Fizzing across its entire visual spectrum, an energy field of some kind was opening up directly above it. The Dalek creature went into emergency mode; the fusion between its physical brain and the mass of technological assistance available to it was immediately being supplied with maximum adrenalin and processor speeds. Super-fast decisions had to be made. Data records instantly accessed from its memory bank showed the most likely match for the phenomenon unfolding above it was… a space-time warp.

Immediate conclusion: something was attacking Carthedia, arriving from another space-time location.

'Emergency! Emergency!' the Dalek instinctively squawked, beaming this message down all its internal comms network transmitters, informing every Dalek in the area. 'Space-time warp materialisation—'

But suddenly it stopped speaking and transmitting. The space warp was mutating into a cascade of freezing, falling objects, hurling themselves through a darkened void towards the Dalek. Data records instantly accessed from its memory bank showed the most likely match: comets. Comets were on a collision course with Carthedia.

But then, before the Dalek could sound the alert about this, three gigantic planets heaved impossibly into view. One was orange, one blue and the other a dazzling rainbow mix – all were pulsing with light of such intensity that the Dalek felt itself thrown into utter confusion.

Abandoning all attempts at accurately identifying the threat, it simply squawked, 'General alert! General alert! Under attack! Under attack!'

It immediately started firing its gun wildly; discharging full power beams, re-angling its gun, firing, re-angling, firing again and again and again in quick succession.

Hellic Dansard was feeling the charge of excitement from the sure and certain knowledge that his irritating ex-client was about to be apprehended. Hellic had never been on a police operation before, and he was starting to find this one pretty thrilling.

A whole squad of police skimmers were accompanying the skimmer in which he was flying. They were swooping down to the spaceport. The Doctor and the children would be hopelessly outnumbered. It would be a very easy arrest. And this time, he would make sure the Doctor was searched for offensive devices that had the capability to knock walls down!

His reputation would be saved and his career put back on track. No nasty surprises this time.

Then everything went wrong.

The skimmer shook violently as something impacted on it.

'What the hell?' screamed one of the policemen as the dashboard exploded in a shower of sparks. 'We've been hit! By what?'

Panic-stricken, Hellic looked out of the windscreen and through the windows all around the skimmer. Screeching up towards them from ground level were flashes of energy, seemingly fired at random. To the left, one of them caught a nearby police skimmer front and centre. The entire vehicle burst into a crackling mass of piercing blue light, with the officers inside horribly illuminated like X-ray images, their mouths wide open in silent screams of agony drowned out by the explosion.

Hellic could see that all the other skimmers were peeling off and flying away as fast as they could. He noticed, however, that his skimmer was rapidly losing height. The thrum of the engine had stopped. They were free falling.

The policemen were flicking switches and pressing buttons, but to no avail.

All at once, the thought struck Hellic that this might well be the end of his chances of promotion.

The Dalek guard by the TARDIS was still firing wildly into the air as the Doctor's stolen skimmer came into land just a few feet away from the gigantic Dalek saucer, expertly piloted by young Ollus Blakely. The doors immediately opened.

'Well done, Ollus!' said the Doctor, leaping out and getting his bearings.

'General alert! General alert!' the Dalek was squawking, more and more agitatedly.

Jenibeth stood close to the Doctor, pulling at his trouser leg.

'Why's it gone bonkers?' she asked.

'I did something clever,' said the Doctor.

'With Ollus's spaceship?' asked Sabel.

'Yes,' said the Doctor, already trying to work out

how they were going to get into the TARDIS. It was directly behind the Dalek. The trouble was, the Dalek was, indeed, behaving as if it were 'bonkers'. It seemed to be almost shadow-boxing with an invisible opponent, moving back and forth and side to side, swivelling its dome and waving its eyestalk around crazily, firing its gun upwards, spraying energy beams in all directions. Even though it was clearly thoroughly occupied and not at all likely to notice them, creeping round it to get into the TARDIS was going to be tricky. There was the danger, for instance, that it might suddenly reverse into them or accidentally blast them with its gun.

At that moment, another police skimmer came screaming out of the sky and thudded into the Dalek. Both exploded on impact, the Dalek screeching a high-pitched squawk as its casing burst open into thousands of white hot fragments.

'Down!' screamed the Doctor, dragging the children as fast as he could behind the huge curved hull of the parked Dalek saucer. He crashed to the landing-pad floor with them just in time, as debris from the explosion smashed into their skimmer. The shrapnel whistled past, superheating the air around it. The Doctor felt a couple of near misses just above his hair and grasped the children as tightly and as close as he could, shielding them with his body.

Fairly quickly, the cacophony subsided and the Doctor stood bolt upright, pulling the children up with him. Their own skimmer was distinctly shredded; but there was almost nothing left of the Dalek or indeed the skimmer that had crashed into it.

'That was… lucky,' said the Doctor, breathlessly. 'About time we had some luck. Thought I'd run out of it for a moment there.'

Jenibeth screamed. The Doctor winced. 'What's the mat—' he began.

'That's not!' said Sabel, pointing to a walkway beyond the landing pad.

'Not what?' asked the Doctor as he followed her gaze. 'Oh.'

'Not lucky,' said Ollus.

A whole squad of Daleks was heading towards them.

'Halt! You are our prisoners!' screamed the Squad Leader. 'You have trespassed on Dalek sovereign territory! Halt!'

'Dalek sovereign…?' mumbled the Doctor, scoffing at such a term. 'What a load of rubbish.' He raised his voice to them. 'You don't fool me, you know!'

'Are we going to get into your crate?' asked Ollus, gently cradling his beloved toy spaceship.

'Yes, come on,' said the Doctor, leading them across the landing pad, past the smouldering debris and towards the inviting blue doors of his ship.

'Hadn't we better hurry?' asked Sabel.

'Nah,' said the Doctor. 'We're standing right in front of a Dalek flying saucer. They won't risk damaging that.'

Suddenly, several scorching beams of energy tore through the air and exploded into the saucer hull, just a few feet away from them.

'Blimey, they *are* in a mood today!' cried the Doctor as he suddenly started sprinting, dragging the children with him. 'Come ooooon!'

And they ran for their lives, beams shooting past them as every Dalek in the squad opened fire. Impacts seared across the landing pad, ruptured the concrete surface, sent chunks of dust and debris into the air. Direct hits to the saucer tore open the outer plating of its hull, ripping the ship apart.

The Doctor and the children rolled and scrambled their way to safety. All the while, the thought pounded through the Doctor's mind... Have I miscalculated this time? Is this how it ends? A stupid bit of over-confidence on some depressing human colony planet where everyone thought the Daleks were the good guys?

Miraculously, they made it to the TARDIS and slammed themselves against it, hiding from the barrage of Dalek fire. The police box shuddered and shook as beams impacted on the other side of it, crackling and spitting like a collision of iced water and white hot larva, the sharp smell of relentless combustion stinging the nostrils.

The children got their breath back, but then all three of them looked confused.

'How come the Dalek guns aren't affecting your crate?' asked Sabel, straining to be heard over the terrible noise.

'She's indestructible!' said the Doctor, patting the TARDIS... which shuddered again as another eardrum-splitting impact slammed into it. 'Well, more or less.'

The trouble was, they couldn't stay hidden here indefinitely, reasoned the Doctor, because the Daleks were getting closer and closer. The angle of their fire was getting wider and wider and soon the beams would reach them, even on this side of the TARDIS. Worse still...

'Oh great! The doors are on the other side!' shouted the Doctor. He was, of course, referring to the side that was currently being blasted.

Suddenly having an idea, the Doctor fixed all three children in turn with the sternest look he could muster. 'Stay here!' he said. 'You understand me?'

They all nodded.

'No matter what happens... *you – don't – move!* Understand?'

They all nodded again.

'Right,' he said, and crouched down, daring to poke his head around to the side of the TARDIS that was being bombarded with deadly rays. He immediately ducked back to the safe side, as several blasts impacted close enough to singe his eyebrows.

'Ow!' he cried out, more for effect than anything else. 'When I need my eyebrows trimming,' he shouted out to the Daleks, 'I'll let you know!' He bit his thumbnail and slapped his hand against the shell of the TARDIS in frustration.

'Are you going to have another plan?' asked Ollus's little voice, barely audible above the screaming Dalek onslaught.

Of course he was going to have another plan. That's what he did! And what's more, thought the Doctor, all of a sudden, it was going to be the *same* plan.

'Give me your spaceship again, please, Ollus,' asked the Doctor, holding out his hand.

Ollus shook his head.

Sabel gave him a sharp look. 'Ollus, be a good boy! The Doctor is having a plan!'

'I let him have my spaceship already today, I did!' protested Ollus. 'He can't have it again. He might break it!'

'Ah, but you didn't see what I did with it, did you?' asked the Doctor, trying to sound as tantalisingly interesting as possible.

'No,' said Ollus and turned his back on the Doctor, folding his arms, keeping the little toy inside his jumper.

'You just fiddled with it and your magic wand and then did a clever thing to the skimmer controls,' offered Jenibeth.

'Er... yes, that's right,' said the Doctor, slightly wrong-footed. 'But wouldn't you like to know exactly what that clever thing was?'

The three children all turned and faced the Doctor. Ollus was considering, his nose wrinkled and his mouth squidging from side to side. Sabel was anxious, clearly aware of the encroaching beams. Jenibeth was full of enthusiasm.

'Oooh, yes please,' said Jenibeth, as if she were volunteering for an extra piece of birthday cake. 'Go on, Ollus, give the Doctor your spaceship again.'

Ollus was still considering.

The searing beams were getting closer. Sabel edged away from the blasts. The Doctor ran his fingers through his hair, trying not to look tense, starting to worry that they might all be fried alive by deadly Dalek death-rays simply because a 4-year-old boy had got into a mood!

Not exactly the least humiliating thing to have on your tombstone, he thought...

'Tell me the clever thing you did before,' said Ollus, coming to a conclusion.

'And then will you give me your spaceship?' asked the Doctor, now really trying his utmost not to sound cross or scared.

'Er... probably,' said Ollus, giving a little shrug.

'Oh, Ollus! We're going to d—' Sabel screamed.

The Doctor raised a placating hand. 'No need to frighten anyone, Sabel,' he said, as calmly as he could. Then he gathered his thoughts for a light-speed explanation of the 'clever thing' he had done. 'OK... Well, it's like this... I-adjusted-the-hologram-projector-of-your-toy-and-the-radio-wave-transmitter-of-the-skimmer. I-transmitted-the-holograms-from-your-toy-directly-at-that-Dalek-on-its-command-frequency... Which-meant-it-ended-up-thinking-it-could-see-space-warps-and-comets-and-big-colourful-planets. In short, it thought it was under attack from something it couldn't understand. What do you say to that?'

Ollus nodded, smiling a big smile. He immediately handed over the toy spaceship to the Doctor. 'That was great,' he said. 'Are you going to do it again?'

The Doctor was already at work with his sonic screwdriver, clicking the controls and provoking various buzzes and bleeps. 'Sort of,' he said, concentrating hard. He flicked a glance to the edge of the safe side of the TARDIS. It was fizzing with burning energy. The beams were starting to move round the corner. The Daleks would soon be able to get a direct shot at them.

He could see that Sabel was fully aware of this. She stared right into his eyes with a fierce combination of fear and hope that was as tangible as a scream for help. He nodded at her, darting his eyes to Jenibeth and Ollus. Sabel, bright as a button, took the hint and gathered her brother and sister into her little arms, hugged them tight and edged them sideways, as far from danger as she dared.

'All right!' said the Doctor, completing his work. 'Same as before... no matter what happens, you stay here!'

He pointed the little toy up at the light on top of the TARDIS. Activating the spaceship and the sonic screwdriver at the same time, he tensed, hoping that he had got his adjustments right. There would be no time left to readjust anything now.

For several, excruciating moments, nothing seemed to happen. Sabel and the children fixed their eyes on him. The Doctor kept pointing the toy at the TARDIS's light, willing it to work with all his might. Sabel gave a little, desperate smile of crumbling encouragement.

Then, just when the Doctor was convinced he had failed and tears were starting to flood down Sabel's face...

A beautiful funnel of compressed, swirling, rainbow light leapt out from the toy towards the top of the TARDIS. As it hit the glass of the TARDIS's lamp, it blossomed into a plume of burgeoning colour, refracting wildly. Then, with a sparkling, dazzling flash, the sky around them was suddenly filled with a huge, holographic projection of space warps, comets, planets, all swirling around each other in a giddying, spectacular display.

The approaching Dalek Squad Leader knew now that it would be mere moments before the Doctor and the children would be visible and in range. The squad's approach had taken them across a vast distance of walkways. They had been under orders to approach at ground level and to maintain a steady, slow course. It did not know why these oddly cautious tactics had been specified, nor did it dare to question. It obeyed. And soon that obedience would be rewarded, it felt sure, with the extermination of the Doctor.

Then...

Nothing seemed to make sense.

Suddenly, a giant space warp was opening up in front of the squad.

A space warp.

Comets thundered towards them.

Gigantic, multi-coloured planets...

For a moment, the Squad Leader and its squad were frozen in indecision. They came to a halt and stopped firing.

All at once, the Doctor suddenly remembered he had succeeded... in the first part of the plan, at least. Now, he, realised, he was wasting precious seconds staring in awe at the beautiful holograms all around.

'Remember... *stay!*' he shouted to the children, as he dashed round the other side of the TARDIS, already brandishing his key.

This side of the TARDIS was still glowing a little from the Dalek gun-blasting it had been receiving. The Doctor noted that the outer shell was even feeling a trifle warm as he thrust the key into the lock and opened the door, dashing inside. Most unusual for the TARDIS. The old girl had really been getting a right pasting, he thought.

The door slammed shut behind him.

Behind the TARDIS, Sabel, Ollus and Jenibeth stayed crouched together.

'Where's he gone?' asked Jenibeth.

'Sssh,' said Sabel. 'Just stay still. You heard what he said.'

'Is he going to come back?' asked Ollus.

'Of course he is!' said Sabel, perhaps a little more angrily than she had intended. And suddenly she found herself questioning her faith in the Doctor. She didn't really know him. He was just a strange man who'd told her that her Mummy and Daddy were dead. He may not even really be a nice man. He may really be horrible. Perhaps he was never coming back.

The Dalek Squad Leader's internal systems had assessed what was happening.

'Threat identified as holographic projection!' it squawked out loud as it transmitted instructions to its fellow Daleks. 'Advance! Recommence firing!'

Sabel, Ollus and Jenibeth instinctively ducked at the sound of the Dalek guns crackling back into life again.

The blue crate shuddered violently under the multiple impacts and Sabel feared the worst. Where was the Doctor? He had gone around the other side of this strange blue crate, and now it was being roasted by the Daleks.

What if the Doctor hadn't managed to open the doors of the crate in time? Would she care if he had died? Would it hurt her as much as the news of her parents' death? Would it even matter? If the Doctor was dead or even just not coming back...

The searing beam impacts fizzed fully round the corner of the TARDIS and started sizzling across the blue, wooden-looking surface.

Sabel immediately dragged Ollus and Jenibeth with her as she struggled to get to safety. But there was nowhere safe to go. There were Dalek beams hitting three sides of this crate, and now they were advancing across the fourth side towards them.

Suddenly, there was another sound. A weird, deep, groaning sound. She remembered she had heard something a bit like it before, when she and her brother and sister had been hiding in the escape pod back on the ship. The sound grew and grew, the groaning roaring into a deep, scraping sound that made her teeth vibrate. It was coming from the blue crate... the Doctor's TARDIS was making this noise.

Sabel turned to the TARDIS and stared at it. To her horror, for an instant, she was beginning to be able to see right through it. The Doctor had said this was what he had arrived on their ship in. This must be the way it travelled. It disappeared, like magic, then reappeared somewhere else. And now… he was leaving them. Leaving them to die.

Then, all of a sudden, the groaning sound crashed to a halt in a gigantic thud and the blue crate was solid again.

By now, Sabel realised, Ollus and Jenibeth were staring at the blue crate too.

'It's changed,' said Ollus, simply.

'What?' asked Sabel. Ollus was a very clever little boy, but this meant that he often said very silly things.

'Oh, for goodness sake, Ollus,' started Sabel – but then she saw what he meant.

The wall of the TARDIS had indeed changed. There were now two circles on it underneath its windows. A small, silver, metal circle and a white, painted, circular symbol.

But before Sabel had a chance to work out what this meant, the blue panelled walls of the TARDIS opened and there stood the Doctor, beaming, arms wide. He had somehow turned this crate around so that the doors were facing them.

The Doctor reached out, grabbed them all and pulled them inside. The doors slammed shut behind them.

Chapter Seven
Dangerous Decision

The cold, blue light of the Dalek Time Controller's eye lens stared intently at the shifting images of eternity. With an expertise honed over centuries, through its dark odyssey stretching across the entirety of space and time, it pinpointed the next moment at which intervention into the Doctor's time stream would be necessary.

Its gunstick twitched, instinctively, as it observed the Doctor pulling the Blakely children inside his TARDIS. It would soon be time…

'Soon…' it murmured to itself.

The Doctor dashed up the steps to the TARDIS console, leaving the children standing at the door. They would need time to adjust, he knew that.

As he busied himself at the controls, effecting an immediate dematerialisation, he afforded himself a glance at Sabel, Ollus and Jenibeth. They looked dumbstruck.

Ollus stepped forward, with purpose, walking up the

stairs. The Doctor wondered exactly what penetrating question about the nature of the TARDIS was about to issue forth from this remarkable 4-year-old.

'Can I have my spaceship back now, please?' asked Ollus.

'Ah...' said the Doctor, plunging a hand into his inside jacket pocket. Ollus looked troubled for a moment or two, until the Doctor produced his spaceship. 'There we are,' said the Doctor, depositing the toy into Ollus's outstretched hands.

Ollus wandered around the console, looking it up and down. The glass spheres inside the central column were now bobbing up and down in time to the grating, scraping sound of the TARDIS engines.

'What's that noise?' asked Ollus. 'Is something going wrong?'

'Er, no!' said the Doctor, defensive and a little hurt. 'Look, let's not mess about here... It's bigger on the inside... much bigger! And it's a time and space machine, which, yes, does mean that we can travel anywhere in time and space. I think that about covers it.'

He looked at the children, taking in each of their expressions in turn. He couldn't quite work out what their reaction was. They looked back at him. Jenibeth tugged at Sabel's arm, pulling her up the steps to the console, following Ollus. They all looked around at the controls. Ollus leaned over to touch a lever.

The Doctor made an urgent, sucking noise with his mouth. Ollus moved away from the lever.

'Sorry,' he said simply. But, the Doctor thought, this little boy was clearly deep in thought.

The children exchanged looks. For all the world, it looked as though they were in some kind of telepathic communication. Which they weren't, thought the Doctor. That would be impossible. But all the same, they seemed to come to some kind of unspoken agreement between them. Jenibeth nudged Sabel closer to the Doctor. Clearly, the eldest girl had been elected spokesperson.

'If this is a time machine...' started Sabel.

Then it struck the Doctor what was coming next. He felt a pang in his hearts. His eyes closed and he put a hand to his face as he turned away from the children. Of course, of course, *of course!* He had brought three children into his TARDIS. Three children who had just lost their parents... in the recent past. And he had told them that they were in a *time machine!*

The Doctor turned back to them.

'No,' he said, simply, and then busied himself with the controls on the console. He was not doing anything in particular, just trying to *look* busy. Trying to look at anything other than the children.

Sabel moved to his side and tugged at his jacket sleeve.

'Won't you even listen to what I have to say?' she asked him.

The Doctor gave a long, long sigh. An outward breath that heaved with the experience of many lifetimes. He found he could still not look at her.

'Doctor?' she said in a tiny, frail voice. He could tell that she was starting to cry; but he could not bear to look at her.

This was the bad side of time travel. There was so much wonder, so many limitless possibilities, so much sheer... adventure and joy. But then there was also this. The terrible tricks of history that any sane person would want to see undone. Since the death of all loved ones causes so much terrible pain, if you have a time machine and could go back and stop that pain... Then why not do it?

The Doctor could still hear Sabel's crying. And when a big sister cries, he thought, so would her little brother and sister. He was right. He could hear Ollus and Jenibeth start to sob.

Here he was, thought the Doctor. The man who could bring empires to their knees, stand up to and defeat the most terrible creatures the universe had to offer... And when it came to children crying, his arsenal of rhetoric, ingenuity and witty reposts was utterly bare. For a moment, all he wanted to do was run away. How could he tell the children he couldn't go back and save their parents?

All at once, the Doctor found himself standing by the TARDIS doors, his back still to the children, his hands over his ears. In that moment, his instinct to get away from the problem had driven him away like a reflex reaction. He must have dashed down the steps, holding his ears. But he had no recollection of doing it.

A little ashamed of himself, he spun round and faced the children. They were looking at him from the control platform, almost in disbelief, their eyes wet with tears.

'Where were you going?' asked Ollus.

'Where was I going?' said the Doctor. 'No idea. Don't

worry. It's pretty usual for me. Sorry about that.'

He looked down at his toes, not really knowing what else to say. Then, without warning, Ollus suddenly blurted out the words the Doctor had not wanted to hear.

'If this is a time machine, we can go back and stop Mummy and Daddy from dying.'

The Doctor looked at them. He saw hope in their eyes. A desperate, ragged hope. It felt like it was smothering him.

'I... can't,' he said. 'I just can't.'

Jenibeth collapsed into sobbing again. She fell to the floor, sitting at the top of the stairs. Sabel knelt by her side, hugging her tightly, staring at the Doctor.

'Why not?' asked Ollus, who, in this instant, seemed more confused than upset. 'Doesn't your machine work properly?'

'Er... well, mostly it does,' said the Doctor. 'Yes, yes, it does!' he corrected himself, feeling defensive again. 'But... well...' How could he say this? 'There are rules.'

'What rules?' asked Ollus.

Of course Ollus was going to ask this. He would just go on and on asking, wouldn't he? He was a child. That's what children do, thought the Doctor. He was going to have to tell him everything.

'My people—' started the Doctor.

'*Your* people?' asked Sabel, her eyes filled with incomprehension. 'Who are *your* people?'

'It...' The Doctor faltered. All this explaining! Explaining felt like the worst thing ever. 'It doesn't matter, they're dead. But my people had rules about this sort of thing. You can't just take people back in time to change things.'

'Why not?' sobbed Jenibeth, looking up at the Doctor, accusingly.

'Because you could bump into yourselves!' said the Doctor, a little too harshly, he thought. 'Sorry,' he added. 'It's all very... timey-wimey and complicated.' He tried a confused smile, hoping for some sympathetic understanding from the children. Then he realised how silly that hope had been.

'Look,' the Doctor tried again. 'If we go back and save your parents, then they may never send the distress call, so I won't have come back to save you. So then, we won't be able to go back and...' The Doctor ran out of steam as he saw Jenibeth and Sabel slowly starting to look away from him. Like the shock of their parents dying had just happened all over again.

'I see...' muttered Ollus, in a remarkably adult fashion.

'Sorry,' said the Doctor again, feeling rather helpless and inadequate. 'What do you see?' he found himself asking, unable to suppress his curiosity about the little boy's response.

'If you do things in the past, you could break the future,' said Ollus. 'Daddy read me a story... *Souder Thunda*, it was.'

'Souder?' the Doctor wondered, almost to himself.

'Some men went back to see the dinosaurs on Earth, and they ruined it,' said Ollus, as if that explained everything. And in a way, it did. The Doctor realised Ollus was talking about *A Sound of Thunder* by a human science fiction writer called Ray Bradbury, in which a safari back to Earth's prehistory had caused Earth's entire history to be rewritten. These truly were the children of great scientists, thought the Doctor.

'Daddy never read *me* that story,' said Sabel, accusingly. 'Why does one silly story make it all right not to bring them back to life?'

'Or the rules of a race long gone…?' muttered the Doctor to himself.

'Who's gone?' asked Jenibeth, barely hearing the Doctor.

The Doctor was thinking fast now, feeling a hotness around his neck. It was that feeling of taking a terrible risk, of leaping into the unknown, of maybe making a huge mistake… But the trouble was, it appealed to him. The death of Alyst and Terrin Blakely had been more or less caused by the Daleks. The Doctor had heard their distress call and had tried to respond. But the TARDIS had been somehow pushed off course by… something. What was that something? *Who* was that something?

Someone was interfering. Someone was *already* interfering in the timeline. Two wrongs didn't make a right, but if the Doctor was up against a situation where the so-called rules of time were already being manipulated and abused, maybe any manipulation of events by him would be no worse.

'Maybe,' the Doctor found himself thinking out loud.

'Maybe what?' asked Sabel, starting to move down the stairs towards the Doctor.

He found he could say no more, because it felt like he was holding a terrible secret within him. In fact, he *was* holding a terrible secret. He was going to break the rules. He was going to give these children their parents back. He was going to undo the terrible work the Daleks had done.

He strode up the steps to the console. As he reached the top, Sabel and Jenibeth grabbed his hands. Needing at least one hand free to operate the controls, he quickly pulled Jenibeth up. She threw her arms around his shoulders and hung on, leaving one of his hands free. He started to tap away at some keys on the console. He pulled down a few levers and punched a number of buttons. Already the TARDIS was starting to groan, like an old ship being forced to turn against the wind. A shudder came up from the bowels of its structure. Sabel let go of the Doctor's hand to steady herself. He instantly used the free hand to make further adjustments.

As he pulled at more levers, pushed more buttons, turned more dials and dashed from one panel to the next, still carrying Jenibeth, he was aware that Ollus was dashing up the steps to join them. Like Sabel, he too grabbed hold of the console for support.

A steady, thundering vibration was now building up. The Doctor could feel his teeth vibrating in his head. He glanced at Sabel and Ollus to reassure them, but their faces were filled with intense anticipation and a growing joy. The Doctor slammed home a few more levers and the vibration became almost intolerably vibrant. Deep crashing noises were whooshing around the control room now, as if gigantic gears were smashing into each other. The groaning of the engines had split into two – one high-pitched whine and one deep, grinding roar.

'A sound of thunder!' cried the Doctor, triumphantly.

'What?' asked Jenibeth, very close to his ear.

'Doesn't matter!' said the Doctor, smiling broadly. 'Here we go!'

He had no idea what they would do when they got back in time to the point before Alyst and Terrin took their lives, but he would do something. Something... good. Something that would wrong-foot whatever devilish Dalek plot was already in motion.

But then...

Everything in the TARDIS suddenly fell silent and still.

'Oh no,' whispered the Doctor.

And then it happened. It was almost the same as the enormous shunt that had occurred when he had tried to go to the rescue of Alyst and Terrin... but this time it was a thousand times more powerful.

Some vast pulse of energy hit the TARDIS and now it seemed to the Doctor that his beautiful old ship might tear itself apart.

Chapter Eight

Hogoosta

Hogoosta was proud of his team. He relaxed back onto his three hind legs, his two mouths settling into a satisfied smile as he observed the team going about their work on the gigantic monument before them.

They were an eclectic bunch, fussing about the great structure, carrying out all manner of complex tasks. He had recruited them from planets across the galaxy. Some he had worked with before, others had been recommended to him by other eminent archaeologists... None of them had disappointed. He knew they were the right people to crack the code of the 'Cradle of the Gods' and discover the truth about the function of this ancient slab of almost mystical technology that sat, four-square in the middle of the Gethrian desert.

It might take years, Hogoosta reflected. He knew that. It might take a lifetime. Maybe longer. Maybe others that followed him would have to pick up his work and carry on with it. In that case, he hoped that one day the secrets of the Cradle of the Gods would be uncovered and entrusted to those who best knew how to deal with and honour them. And that was enough for Hogoosta. He was a truly patient creature.

The only part of all this that troubled him was the fact that he feared that the power contained within the Cradle would present a terrible danger to the galaxy. He had explored the cosmos all his long, long life, seeking out the secrets of ancient civilisations and technologies, and he had developed a feel for dormant and awesome power. On a couple of occasions, this had led him to keep his findings secret, for fear of them being exploited by conquest-hungry, unprincipled minds. And he had this fear now.

When he had engaged Alyst and Terrin Blakely, via inter-space communications, to help him with certain physics-related problems vital to the work on Gethria, he had been mightily impressed by their work and was convinced that they were on the verge of unlocking the secrets of the past. Then it occurred to him that the work they had done, transmitted as it was across open space, could so easily fall into the wrong hands. He had immediately told Alyst and Terrin to cease their communication, destroy all physical record of their conclusions and come straight to Gethria to continue their work with him in person. And beware of anyone trying to get the information from them.

That had been some time ago, and now the lack of communication from his friends Alyst and Terrin Blakely was worrying him. They should have arrived on Gethria already. But he dared not investigate, for fear of drawing attention to them and the secrets they carried in their heads.

As to the nature of the real purpose of the Cradle of the Gods… Every day for the past forty-seven years, Hogoosta had pondered that conundrum. And as every year passed, he became more and more certain that the complex, planetary inscriptions on the walls of its inner chambers and the often reported supernatural episodes experienced there were a signal that truly devastating powers were housed within the Cradle.

Hogoosta was not a believer in the supernatural, but he was experienced enough in the field of interplanetary archaeology to know that the unexplained effects of long-dead technologies could sometimes feel like visitations from beyond the grave. He himself had felt it, while alone in the Cradle's inner chambers. That feeling of someone or something else being there with him, when he was certain the chamber was empty. There had been times when the air had felt so thick with the presence of 'something' that he had found himself to be genuinely fearful. He did not speak publicly of these experiences, but he bore them in mind and was convinced that what he was experiencing was the stirring of some unimaginably powerful technology from galactic prehistory. He was determined that one day, if at all possible, he would know its secret. And then, he thought, then he would decide if the modern civilisations of the galaxy were ready to learn about it.

As he gazed up at the soaring tower of the monument, it struck Hogoosta that night was beginning to fall. The sky above the Gethrian wasteland was turning a deep, beautiful purple and the stars were starting to shine through. He eased himself forward, seven upright legs now ready to support him, ready to walk back to the skimmer that would return him and his team to the nearest town, Gesela, where they would rest and replenish themselves before the next day's toil to unearth the Cradle's secrets.

Suddenly, however, the highly sensitive, bone-like ears atop his pyramid-shaped head detected a sound. It was coming from high above, in the sky, and was growing in intensity. It was a spaceship approaching, coming in to land.

Moments later, and his team had picked up on the noise too. All of them downed tools and equipment and joined Hogoosta, staring up into the night sky. There they saw a tiny pinpoint of light growing larger by the second.

It could be Alyst and Terrin, thought Hogoosta, hopefully.

But as the ship got closer, it seemed far too large and military-looking to be a chartered ship transporting two avid physicists and their family. This was a ship with a highly polished surface and signs of weaponry banks bristling across its oval-shaped hull.

Then Hogoosta spotted some familiar markings. It was a ship from his own people, the Klektids. But not necessarily a welcome one. The markings were those of the Klektid Enforcers, an order of Klektid warriors who had, in recent times, hired themselves out to anyone who could afford them. They would enforce the law wherever they were paid to go.

The Enforcer ship touched down with a dusty thud, its landing legs having extended to absorb the impact in large, hydraulic cylinders. A door slid open and a ramp shot down rapidly into the dusty desert floor. Straight away, a squad of Klektid Enforcers scuttled down the ramp, brandishing formidable-looking weapons.

They were indeed the same species as Hogoosta, seven-legged, wide bodies with bony pyramidal heads sitting on top of flexible, extending necks. Except these Klektids, unlike Hogoosta, were clad, not in lightweight, loose-fitting material suitable for hot desert life, but with tight-fitting armour, glinting, metallic.

They made straight for Hogoosta. The self-evident leader of the squad, with ceremonial blue head-dress, extended his neck fully in a gesture designed, Hogoosta knew, to assert authority and intimidate. He peered down at Hogoosta threateningly.

Hogoosta did not respond. He knew there was no point trying to face up to an armed squad of Enforcers. He also knew that failing to respond would annoy the squad leader – which gave him some small satisfaction. But it was to be short-lived.

The leader's bony mouths clicked open and shut rapidly, emitting the characteristic stereo chorus of his species.

'We are shutting down this dig site,' he announced.

Before Hogoosta could utter a word, he heard the crash of other Enforcers pulling down scaffolding erected next to the monument. It was a symbolic gesture of intent, he gathered. As the dust settled, he could see that no one had actually been hurt; but members of his team retreated in alarm and were being ushered towards the awaiting skimmer.

'You are to be evicted from this planet!' said the squad leader.

Now Hogoosta knew for sure that the Cradle of the Gods represented something really dangerous.

The Doctor stepped out of the TARDIS, turning briefly to tell the Blakely children that it might be too dangerous for them to come with him and that he should check things out first. The trouble was, the children had *already* scooted through his legs and under his arms and were *already* running across the desert in the bright moonlight.

'Nooo!' cried the Doctor, in a futile sort of fashion. But it had no effect. 'Who'd be a dad?' he muttered to himself as he ran off to catch the children.

They were well ahead of him, having spotted, he imagined, the lights he had just noticed in the mid-distance. He could hear them giggling and whooping. How changeable they were. How remarkable their ability to live purely in the moment. They had been so relieved when the TARDIS had not actually been torn apart and had finally landed on Gethria that, for a while at least, they seemed to have forgotten the deep pain of the loss of their parents.

The Doctor smiled to himself. 'Resilient,' he said, and then broke into a run to catch them up, which he did easily.

'Whoa! Whoa! Slow down,' he said, placing a gentle hand on Sabel's head. Sabel, in turn, held on to Jenibeth's hand. Jenibeth tried to hold on to Ollus's hand, but he dodged away, simply turning to face the Doctor, pointing at the lights in the distance.

'What is it?' he asked.

'I don't know,' said the Doctor. 'A settlement of some sort, I expect. People probably live there.'

'I thought you said you'd been here before,' said Sabel, slightly accusingly.

'I have, but that was in a different time period,' he explained. 'Things seemed friendly enough then, but who knows what might be here now. Remember, the TARDIS more or less crash-landed.'

'Didn't you land here on purpose?' asked Jenibeth.

'Er... no, no I didn't,' said the Doctor, scratching his head. It was troubling him that the energy pulse from the Vortex had mysteriously propelled him back to the very planet he had visited just before he had landed on the Blakely's spaceship. He felt sure there must be a connection.

'And the truth is,' he said, finding himself thinking aloud, 'I'm feeling more than a little bit manipulated.'

'You mean when everything went wrong in the TARDIS, someone else was making that happen and they wanted you to come here?' asked Sabel.

'Perhaps,' mused the Doctor. 'You'd better stay close. And you'd better be quiet from now on,' he added, a little gruffly. The children looked back at him, clearly a little hurt.

'I'm not telling you off,' the Doctor explained. 'Just... you know, behave yourselves. Aren't you afraid of the dark or anything?'

'Daddy said being afraid of the dark was stupid,' said Ollus.

'Oh,' said the Doctor. 'Not entirely sensible of him.'

As they reached the outskirts of the small settlement, the Doctor could see by the dim light of Gethria's three or four moons that its dusty streets were packed with activity. Creatures of all kinds were running along between the low, stone buildings. There were squeals and frantic vocalisations of all kinds. Many of the aliens were clutching what looked like valued items to themselves, quite often more items than could comfortably be carried.

'This is an evacuation,' the Doctor murmured to himself.

'Evacu-shon?' asked Ollus.

'The people are leaving,' explained Sabel. 'That's right, isn't it, Doctor?'

'I think so,' said the Doctor slowly as he put his arms around the children, sensing danger and starting to crouch down.

Suddenly, one of the creatures in the settlement stopped, turned its pyramidal head and shot a look straight at them.

'Ah,' said the Doctor. 'Busted.'

The creature scuttled towards them, very probably as fast as it could move, its seven bony legs kicking up a minor dust storm as it approached. One of its four arms was carrying a metallic item that was unmistakably a weapon.

As it came to a halt in front of them, its long neck

extending so that its strange face was peering down at them, Ollus shouted out, 'Hogoosta Funny-Legs!'

The creature immediately pointed its weapon directly at Ollus. The Doctor instinctively thrust himself in front of the boy, blocking him from the creature's view.

'We're not getting off to a very good start, are we?' said the Doctor, his voice low and more than a little threatening. 'Perhaps we should politely introduce each other? Eh? What do you say to that?'

'Who are you?' asked the creature, stereophonically, from its two mouths, jerking its gun and extending its neck even higher. By the blinking of its eyes, the Doctor imagined this extra extension was causing it some discomfort. Served it right!

'Now you're just not listening, are you?' continued the Doctor, inching towards the creature, his posture becoming ever more threatening. 'But for your information, I am the Doctor. And for your *further* information, I'm never really impressed by people whose opening gambit in a conversation is to point a gun at a child's head!'

Those final words rang out loud and clear as the Doctor allowed himself to lose his temper a little. The creature involuntarily jerked back a little. Glancing over its shoulder, the Doctor noticed that some of the activity in the settlement had ceased. His voice had carried and a few of the bustling creatures had stopped to see what all the noise was about.

'He looks just like Hogoosta Funny-Legs,' came the muffled voice of Ollus from behind the Doctor's tweed jacket. This was quickly followed by a 'Sssh!', from Sabel, the Doctor guessed.

'So, you're a Klektid, then?' the Doctor said. 'But clearly not Hogoosta Funny-Legs.'

'Hogoosta Fun—' The creature corrected itself. 'Hogoosta is the head of the Archaeological Dig Site which is being evicted from this planet.'

'Oh, really,' mused the Doctor. 'By you, I assume. You and your big gun. That right, is it?'

The Doctor put a disparaging finger on the weapon. The Klektid withdrew the weapon sharply.

'And the aforementioned Hogoosta is here!' came another voice from behind the threatening Klektid.

The Doctor and the children moved as one; taken aback by the sudden, surreptitious arrival of someone else. The Klektid with the gun turned round to reveal another Klektid creature behind it. Its features were broadly the same, but its clothing was softer, gentler... and there was something far more kindly about its posture and expression.

'Oh, hello, Hogoosta,' said the Doctor, feigning familiarity for what he believed was the best.

The children jumped and yelped with delight. 'Hogoosta Funny-Legs!' they cried. The Doctor put his arms out to hold them back. He stared hard at the new arrival... at Hogoosta. The kinder Klektid face softened further. The Doctor was becoming fairly sure he could trust this Hogoosta person.

'They're with me!' Hogoosta said firmly to the Klektid holding the gun. It surveyed him from above, then slowly lowered its extended neck. The Doctor thought he spotted a little relief on the aggressive Klektid's odd face. That neck stretching business must have taken it out of him a bit.

'Continue your evacuation!' the Klektid barked out as it turned and scuttled away back to the settlement.

At this, the children broke free of the Doctor's restraining arms and ran to Hogoosta. He greeted them warmly, extending his four arms around them and allowing Ollus to clamber up his body, using two of his legs as supports. They had clearly created quite a bond during their many inter-space communications with each other.

'Children! It is so good to see you!' said Hogoosta. He glanced at the Doctor. The Doctor looked straight into Hogoosta's eyes and he could tell by the creature's gentle shift in expression that it knew something was wrong.

Sabel was too smart to have missed this.

'Mummy and Daddy are dead,' she said, simply. Ollus and Jenibeth immediately fell silent and bowed their heads. Hogoosta's tender grip on them tightened a little and his pyramidal head vibrated slightly, like a shudder of emotion was running up that strange, long neck.

The Doctor nodded in sad confirmation.

'And who is this?' asked Hogoosta, gesturing to the Doctor with a free arm.

'He's the Doctor,' said Jenibeth.

'He saved us,' Ollus added, straight away. Jenibeth and Sabel both nodded.

'And he's very, very clever,' said Jenibeth.

The five of them stood there for a moment or two, in silence, not knowing quite what to say or do next. There was so much yet to find out, the Doctor knew that. But where to start?

'Come with me,' said Hogoosta.

Chapter Nine
The Cradle Awakens

The Doctor sat, slightly uncomfortably, in Hogoosta's small stone house. He was sitting on a chair no doubt perfectly designed for the comfort of a Klektid. For someone with only two legs, it was decidedly... lumpy.

The children sat silently. Sabel was leaning on a table leg. Jenibeth lay on the floor with her head in Sabel's lap, as Sabel gently ran her fingers through Jenibeth's hair. Ollus was quietly playing with his toy spaceship again.

Hogoosta had just finished explaining the Cradle of the Gods to the Doctor, and telling him how the Klektid Enforcers were shutting down the dig site. This, Hogoosta said he felt sure, meant that the secret technological purpose of the Cradle of the Gods was something dangerous. The Doctor nodded slowly in agreement.

Outside, the bustle of the eviction from Gethria was continuing. Every now and then, Hogoosta gave a wary glance out of the stone-framed window, and tidied away more of his belongings into a large, leathery bag.

'It won't be long before they ship us out now,' he said.

Everyone turned to the Doctor. He was deep in thought and remained silent for a good few seconds. Finally, he spoke.

'Why's it called the Cradle of the Gods?' he asked.

'No one knows for certain,' confessed Hogoosta. 'But several possible translations of some of the hieroglyphics inside the inner chamber hint at the… well…' He paused, clearly troubled by the thought. 'The creation or destruction of planets.'

'I see,' said the Doctor. 'Creation *or* destruction?'

'Depending on the translation,' said Hogoosta, shrugging all four arms.

'Tricky business, this translation lark, isn't it?' mused the Doctor. 'And you think your Klektid Enforcers are interested in getting their hands on this power to create… or destroy?'

'No,' said Hogoosta. 'The Enforcers just do the bidding of the highest payer.' Then he moved in closer to the Doctor, clearly rattling his mouths as quietly as he could. 'What exactly happened to Alyst and Terrin?'

The children were, the Doctor knew, unfortunately still able to overhear.

'The Daleks,' he said, barely louder than a whisper.

'The Daleks?' Hogoosta seemed almost amused.

'Oh, don't tell me!' sighed the Doctor. 'You think they're a force for good, for progress… the Sunlight Worlds etcetera, etcetera… Am I right?'

'Well…' Hogoosta shrugged again, his strange

interlocking arm bones moving in sequence, creating a sort of wave effect.

'Oh come off it, Hogoosta,' said the Doctor. 'You're an archaeologist. You know about the past. Surely you've heard about the Daleks and what they've done.'

'I have,' confessed the Klektid. 'But that was long ago. And their more recent works speak for themselves.'

'Oh do they? Do they indeed?' said the Doctor, rolling his eyes in frustration and starting to lose his temper a little. 'It's the Daleks who tried to get Alyst and Terrin to give up their secret. They threatened to board their ship. They were very insistent. So insistent that poor Alyst and Terrin felt the only way to preserve their secret was to…'

He stopped short, flicking a look to the children.

Hogoosta seemed to understand. 'I see…' he clicked, slowly, through only one mouth. 'I see…' His head shuddered again, indicating, the Doctor felt sure, that he was moved by the thought of this.

'So,' continued the Doctor, more stridently now. 'I have to find out what this Cradle of the Gods actually does and make sure the Daleks don't get hold of it. Actually, on second thoughts… I've mostly just got to make sure the Daleks don't get hold of it. Finding out what it does would just be the icing on the cake. So, Hogoosta, you'd better get us there, now.'

'I can't,' said Hogoosta.

'What do you mean, you can't?' asked the Doctor, a little petulantly. Then he moved in closer to Hogoosta and whispered, 'No such word as can't.'

'The Enforcers won't let us go back to the dig site.'

'Then we'll just have to go there without their permission!' said the Doctor standing up to make his fearless pronouncement, accidentally knocking the chair down behind him. 'Sorry…' he muttered, picking the chair back up again and setting it right. 'So, let's go!'

The darkness of the night sky on Gethria was just showing the first tinges of lightening up for morning as the Doctor, Hogoosta, Sabel, Jenibeth and Ollus made their dash across the desert towards the Cradle of the Gods. Hogoosta was leading, all seven legs powering as fast as they could go.

It was difficult for the Doctor to keep up. He was impressed by Hogoosta's strength, especially since Sabel and Jenibeth were holding on tight to the Klektid's bony torso. Ollus had insisted on sitting upon the Doctor's shoulders, which was largely *why* the Doctor was finding it difficult to keep up.

Right next to his ear, the Doctor could hear the irritating buzzing and bleeping of Ollus's toy spaceship.

'Don't you ever stop playing with that thing?' asked the Doctor sharply, twisting his neck momentarily to squint back at Ollus.

'It was my Daddy's,' said Ollus, concentrating on the spaceship.

The Doctor said no more. This was all the poor boy had left of his father. Let him play with it whenever he liked.

The Doctor glanced back over his other shoulder and was somewhat dismayed by what he saw.

'We've got trouble!' he called across to Hogoosta.

Hogoosta's head spun round 360 degrees. 'They were bound to miss us soon enough,' he said. 'I told you.'

Behind them, the Doctor could see the rising dust of what must have been the Klektid Enforcers pursuing them.

'We'll never make it there before they catch us up,' said Hogoosta.

'Then we'd better make a diversion,' replied the Doctor.

As they carried on running, the Doctor checked his sonic screwdriver. He felt Ollus's legs clamp more firmly around his neck, trying to stop himself from falling off.

The screwdriver bleeped as the Doctor set it into homing mode. He immediately detected which way they had to head to get to the TARDIS. Luckily, it wasn't much of a deviation in their route, and it was fairly close by.

'Come on! This way!' called the Doctor, bearing left a little and pulling ahead.

Hogoosta and his cargo of Sabel and Jenibeth followed. As they pounded on across the sand and the morning light crept further into the sky, the Doctor could hear his hearts thudding with exhaustion and feel perspiration trickling down his face. Slowing down was not an option, though. Every time he glanced back over his shoulder, the dust trail of the approaching Klektid Enforcers was larger and closer.

Suddenly, something bright and hot shot through the air to their right. It hit the ground and sent up a burst of fire and a shower of burning hot sand.

'They're shooting at us!' shouted Ollus, right into the Doctor's ear.

'I know!' the Doctor shouted back. He squinted through the clearing clouds of the explosion and to his relief, he could see the TARDIS up ahead.

'They've got our range,' cried out Hogoosta. 'They won't hesitate to kill us.'

'Then they're lousy shots,' the Doctor cried.

Another flash. Another explosion hit the ground just ahead of them again.

'Nah!' shouted the Doctor. 'I don't think they're trying to kill us. Just trying to frighten us.'

More flashes and three more explosions ripped into the desert floor around them.

'*I'm* frightened!' shouted Sabel.

The Doctor still did not slacken his pace and Hogoosta was easily matching his speed, starting to overtake him. They were getting ever closer to the TARDIS, but when the Doctor turned again, he could actually see the detail of the Klektid Enforcers themselves. They were clearly much fitter specimens than Hogoosta; trained for combat and not carrying small children.

'What is that thing?' called Hogoosta, pointing to the TARDIS.

'It's mine,' replied the Doctor. 'And it's a safe place for us to hide.'

'Hide?' queried Hogoosta.

'It's huge inside,' cried out Jenibeth. 'And it flies!'

Another four flashes, and the Doctor could feel the explosive heat much closer now. He could also hear the sound of sand showering against the surface of the

TARDIS's outer shell. They were nearly there.

'Look out!' screamed Sabel. The Doctor could see her pointing off to the right, ahead of them.

There was a blur of movement. But as the Doctor squinted at it, he could clearly see several Klektid Enforcers moving off ahead of them, circling around to approach the TARDIS from the rear. Were they being surrounded? Sure enough, more Klektids raced round from the left, heading towards their flank.

At last they arrived, colliding with the locked TARDIS doors. Hogoosta came to a halt at almost exactly the same instant.

'This thing doesn't look like enough protection to—'

The Klektid's words were cut off by another explosion followed by a shower of more burning sand. The smell was peculiarly unpleasant and the hot granules danced off the Doctor's exposed skin like vicious bee stings.

'Argh!' he gasped, and dropped the TARDIS key, just as he was about to insert it into the lock.

Another explosion, and the shower of sand quickly buried the key. As the Doctor bent down to find it, Ollus leapt off his back and started to dig in the sand. Sabel and Jenibeth climbed down from Hogoosta and joined in the search.

'The Doctor must not be allowed to escape in his TARDIS!'

The Doctor twitched round at this shrill Klektid command. A squad of about forty of them was moving in towards them now. But how did they know his name? And how did they know about the TARDIS?

'Here!' shouted Ollus, over the painful din of another

salvo of explosions.

The little boy was holding the key up to him, hand outstretched. Ollus's face had a questioning look on it. A reaction to the Doctor's own face, which must have been a picture of suspicion and dread, he realised.

'Key! Yes!' the Doctor shouted, coming back to his senses. Now, he could hear the footsteps of the Klektids as they approached. He looked around. They were surrounded by an ever-tightening circle of Enforcers.

Without another thought, the Doctor grabbed the key, opened the TARDIS's doors and shoved everyone inside.

He slammed the doors shut behind them all and headed straight up the steps to the TARDIS control console.

'You explain it to him,' the Doctor called back to the children, gesturing to the TARDIS's vast interior, as he busied himself with some adjustments.

'We don't understand it either,' the Doctor heard Sabel saying. 'But isn't it marvellous?'

'It's like magic,' squeaked Jenibeth.

'No, just clever science,' argued Ollus.

The Doctor glanced over and saw Hogoosta's head revolving in confusion. The Klektid was shuddering again.

Ollus ran up the steps towards the Doctor.

'Are we leaving? Are we flying off to another planet in another time?' the little boy asked, miming the trajectory of escaping with his little spaceship and impersonating the TARDIS's engines by making a rhythmic, grating, gurgling sound in his mouth.

'Another time?' asked Hogoosta, mounting the stairs and heading, clattering, towards the Doctor too. His head came to a rest.

'Daren't risk it,' explained the Doctor. 'There's something out there in the Vortex which keeps interfering. So...'

He busied himself with the controls, then grabbed at them, shunting several levers into place with a resolute clunk. The TARDIS made a slight, truncated groaning sound and the entire control room shuddered somewhat, then fell still.

'What did you do?' asked Ollus.

Hogoosta's head started rocking from side to side.

'I cheated a bit,' said the Doctor.

Hogoosta's head stopped rocking. 'Cheated?' he asked.

'Couldn't risk fully entering the Vortex,' explained the Doctor.

'The... Vortex?' asked Hogoosta, his arms flicking around agitatedly.

'So I just did a bit of instantaneous travel,' beamed the Doctor. 'Should give us a slight advantage over your Klektid friends.'

'They are not *my* friends,' said Hogoosta, somewhat indignantly.

'No, no they're not, are they?' agreed the Doctor as he descended the steps. 'But whose friends are they? Eh? That's the question. Anyway...'

And with that, he flung the TARDIS doors open.

The Doctor led them out into what he was sure must

be an underground chamber. It had a cold clamminess about it and no natural light, just half a dozen electric lamps on stands. His sincerest hope was that it was in fact a chamber beneath the so-called Cradle of the Gods. He immediately turned to Hogoosta and asked for confirmation.

'Yes… yes… We are here. The inner chamber,' the Klektid confirmed. 'Amazing. So your… TARDIS? Your TARDIS is a teleportation device.'

The Doctor looked a little indignant and was about to take issue with this slight on his precious ship, but then he remembered how little time they had before the Enforcers would guess this was where they were. He focused his attention on the hieroglyphics, clearly engraved on the walls of this chamber many centuries ago.

'Bit more complicated than that, Hogoosta, old fella,' he muttered absently as he moved his face ever closer to the wall. His nose made contact. He sniffed hard. 'Hmmm… this is ancient. Far too ancient for me to be able to translate.'

He pulled out his sonic screwdriver and whizzed it around, getting a reading.

'Yup. Definitely more ancient than ancient.'

He turned to look at the children and Hogoosta, who were standing with the TARDIS at their back. They were all starting to look around in dumbstruck wonder. Instinctively, he followed their gaze. On first sight, this chamber had looked rather dull to him as he had exited the TARDIS. What was having such an effect on them? And why was Hogoosta looking so incredibly awe-struck, considering he had been looking at this chamber for many years?

Then the Doctor noticed.

Light had started to play all around them, growing in intensity. A kind of whirling, surging light that brought with it a tangible vibration in the air.

'Well, well, well,' breathed the Doctor, looking up at the ceiling. Every single indentation between the impossibly old building blocks of this chamber was tingling with a multicoloured fizz of energy. A fizz that was slowing transmuting into a glow. Then a rumbling started.

'Power...' said the Doctor. He spun round, opening his arms wide. He could feel some sort of energy growing in this space. It felt like it was vibrating his very veins. It was sizzling, burrowing into his mind. Every molecule of matter and air seemed to be alive with it.

'Can't you feel it?' he asked the others. He turned back to look at them all again. He knew they were feeling something, but it looked very much like whatever it was had robbed them of their ability to speak.

Ollus managed to break the spell first. 'Wow...' he murmured in a tiny, breathy voice, still clutching his little spaceship.

Jenibeth rubbed her head. 'Feels funny,' she said in a way that suggested she couldn't decide whether it was funny 'good' or funny 'bad'.

'And this has never happened before, Hogoosta?' the Doctor asked.

'No... never,' said Hogoosta, his mouths starting to click a little out of sync, rendering his speech a touch imprecise. All this was clearly having a deeply felt effect on him. 'I have... have no idea what's... what's going on.'

All of a sudden, the Doctor had an idea.

'Then it's to do with one of us,' he said. 'Not you, Hogoosta. One of us. All of us? Some of us? I'm not sure. Let's take a look upstairs. Hogoosta?'

The Doctor gestured quickly in several possible directions at several possible exits. He hoped Hogoosta would get the hint. Luckily, he did.

'Ah, this way,' said Hogoosta, scuttling through a triangular archway.

The Doctor ushered Ollus, Sabel and Jenibeth after him, all the while his mind racing.

Hogoosta led them all up a wide, spiralling staircase. Spurred on by the Doctor, they ran as fast as they could go, the children once again holding on to adults for support. Ollus clambered up the Doctor again and Sabel and Jenibeth returned to their seated positions on Hogoosta, although it looked like a far more bumpy ride going upstairs.

When they surfaced, the morning had encroached upon the night a little more. But the weak glow from the emerging Gethrian sun was made even more pale and insignificant by the light show that was apparently just beginning on the outer monument structure of the Cradle of the Gods.

It was immediately obvious what had caused the rumble of power. Aside from the shafts of light that were lancing out from the gigantic tower, large slabs of granite-like rock making up the base of it were in the process of moving, apparently of their own volition. A complex series of what the Doctor guessed were predetermined patterns was unfolding before their very eyes. The Cradle of Life was re-sculpting itself into... something.

Something alive with power.

'What are you? What are you? What are you?' murmured the Doctor to himself in awe. 'A power for destruction or creation?'

He started to wonder if they should really be here. If the Cradle's real purpose was destruction, then it would be their presence that would trigger the deployment of some appalling, ancient weapon. And yet, the Doctor's curiosity left him fixed to the spot. Whatever was going on, it was somehow harnessing the elemental forces of the universe. This was truly a spectacle undeniably worthy of inclusion in the pantheon of ancient wonders of the cosmos.

Hogoosta moved to the Doctor's side.

'It's finally happened,' the Klektid's mouths clattered in an almost uncontrollable jumble of sounds, making it necessary for the Doctor to take a few moments to work out what Hogoosta had actually said. 'After all these years... Today is the day.'

They were both distracted by a new, deep thundering, coming from a different direction altogether. Was this it? Was this the weapon activating?

'Doctor!' squealed Sabel over all the noise. 'Look!'

She was pointing up into the sky, away from the monument. The Doctor and Hogoosta looked to where she was pointing.

'It's a ship. Like that Dalek one!' Ollus shouted.

Almost exactly like that Dalek one, thought the Doctor. A Dalek flying saucer was landing close by.

'No chance of that being a coincidence,' said the Doctor.

'Daleks?' asked Hogoosta, confused. 'Why would the Daleks come here?'

'Why indeed?' said the Doctor bluntly. 'Why did they try to get the secret of the Cradle from the Blakelys? How did your Klektid Enforcers know about me and the TARDIS? Eh?'

Hogoosta's head swayed uncertainly.

'Because the Daleks must be paying the Enforcers!' shouted Sabel.

'Yes!' said the Doctor, pointing at her, smiling grimly.

'But...' began Hogoosta, a note of dread in his strange clicking voice. 'The Enforcers are employed by the consortium who fund this project.'

'The Daleks! It's the Daleks who are funding your project, Hogoosta!' said the Doctor.

With an enormous crunching sound and a vast cloud of fast-moving dust, the Dalek ship touched down. The minor sand storm hit hard, showering the transforming monument, dulling the shafts of light emanating from it for a few moments.

The Doctor, spitting dust from his mouth and shielding his eyes with his arm, grabbed the children and held them close to him as best he could. Hogoosta, finally snapping out of his daze, gave the best assistance he could muster too.

As the dust settled, leaving them all spluttering and

smarting from the sting in their eyes, ears and noses, they saw that a hatchway had already opened in the saucer. A ramp had extended downwards and had crashed down upon the baked surface of the desert.

The sun was almost fully risen now, and its rays caught the bronze glint of the Daleks that filed swiftly down the ramp onto the sand. The Doctor squinted hard at them. For a moment, something seemed odd about the leading Dalek. It seemed to blur at its centre for an instant... Then the Doctor remembered when this had happened before. In the courtroom on Carthedia.

'The Dalek Litigator...' he murmured to himself. 'What brings you here?'

But he dismissed the question almost immediately. The Cradle of the Gods was somehow activating and he and the children had something to do with it. The Enforcers had clearly called up the Daleks, very probably having transmitted the image of the Doctor and the children to them. He couldn't let the Daleks get access to this Cradle, whatever it was in the middle of doing. There was only one possible course of action.

'We have to get out of here!' shouted the Doctor, grabbing the children. 'You too, Hogoosta. Trust me, the Daleks can turn pretty nasty when it comes to me. And they've seen you with me.'

The Doctor and the children were already at the entrance to the spiral staircase, about to descend.

'But this is my work,' Hogoosta said, his voice full of pride. 'I cannot just leave.'

'We can come back,' called the Doctor. 'Come on! Trust me, the Daleks won't—'

Before he could finish his words, there was a burning beam of light and a soaring sound, harsh enough to cut through the cacophony of the awakening Cradle. The beam sliced through the air and lanced straight into Hogoosta. For a moment, the Klektid was consumed in a cruel, burning blue light so bright that it momentarily imprinted a negative image across the Doctor's retina.

Hogoosta had been murdered by fire from a Dalek gun.

The children froze in terror. The Doctor, hearing the approaching whine of Dalek motive power, bundled Ollus, Sabel and Jenibeth together, pushing them down the stairs.

'Come on!' he yelled.

As they descended the ancient, worn steps, faltering and tripping over each other, the familiar, repugnant sounds of Dalek speech rang out across the monument.

'Fugitives are to be captured immediately!'

The Doctor was pretty sure that this was the voice of the so-called Dalek Litigator. What kind of Dalek was this? A creature that purported to be in charge of Dalek prosecutions and yet had travelled across half the galaxy to bring the Doctor to book. What exactly was going on here?

As the Doctor and the children reached the bottom of the stairs, the motive power sounds of the Daleks echoing down the stairwell transformed into something even more worrying. The Doctor knew this sound only too well. The Daleks were taking off, flying. They were about to hover down the steps after them.

'Ollus, Sabel, Jenibeth! Come on!' barked the Doctor,

dashing to the TARDIS, unlocking the doors and flinging them open again. He turned to make sure the children were safely on their way… Then his hearts went cold in shock. Where was Jenibeth?

'Jenibeth? Jenibeth, where is she?' he said to Ollus as the little boy passed him.

Sabel had already entered the TARDIS. Ollus turned back to look as he reached the doorway.

And then they both saw that Jenibeth had somehow tripped at the bottom of the stairs.

'Jenibeth!' shouted little Ollus with all his might.

Confused and dazed, Jenibeth staggered bravely to her feet. She rubbed her head and looked down at her grazed knees and started to cry.

Knowing she was too stunned to move quickly enough, the Doctor began to launch himself towards her. But he felt a tiny hand on his sleeve. He looked back. It was Ollus, trying to stop him.

'Ollus?' the Doctor asked, bewildered.

Ollus was staring to where Jenibeth was. The Doctor turned back to look again.

A Dalek had landed right beside Jenibeth. Still dazed, she seemed hardly aware of this deadly killing machine as its suction cup arm extended towards her.

'No!' yelled the Doctor, overwhelmed by a sense of utter futility.

More Daleks landed around Jenibeth.

'It's too late,' said Ollus. 'This is a time machine. You can come back to get her.'

The Doctor could not think of a single word to say that would make sense or help in this situation. When he had foolishly decided to break the Laws of Time before, to try to reunite the children with their parents, he had truly opened a can of temporal worms. The Doctor drew breath, not knowing quite what he was going to say, but—

'We'll come back for you! We'll come back for you! I promise!' Ollus shouted out to Jenibeth, just as the first Dalek's suction cup made contact with her. She let out a confused squeal, suddenly realising she was surrounded.

'Surrender or the girl will be—'

With all his might, Ollus pulled the Doctor into the TARDIS and slammed the doors shut before they could hear the final, fatal word from the Dalek. He turned to the Doctor, leaning his little head on the door, his fingers in his ears, his eyes red with tears.

'We can go back. We can go back. We can go back,' he was almost chanting to himself.

The Doctor reached out to Ollus, still not knowing what to do. He put a reassuring hand on the little boy's head and smiled as best he could. Then he broke away and rushed up the steps to the console. Sabel was already standing there.

'You won't go back, though, will you?' she said.

The Doctor looked at her and, for a moment, felt he could not move.

'Not this time,' she said. 'You won't, will you?'

The Doctor turned away and operated the TARDIS controls. The engines started to heave and the shapes within the central column propelled themselves up and down as the ship dematerialised from Gethria and headed into the Vortex.

The Doctor could hear Ollus's little feet frantically patter up the steps towards him. He tripped just as he reached the top. The Doctor heard him fall and cry out. Sabel ran to the little boy to help him up. Rubbing his shins and fighting back tears, Ollus walked right up to the Doctor.

'You will go back, though, won't you?' he said. 'You were going to do that before, you were.'

'I was,' nodded the Doctor. 'But it's different this time.'

'How is it different?' asked Ollus, starting to get cross.

'Last time, something had pushed the TARDIS and me away from getting to your parents on time. Something or someone had already interfered in the flow of time.'

'So it was all right for you to interfere then, to put that right?' asked Sabel.

'Well…' the Doctor ran a hand through his hair. Why did humans always ask about this? he thought to himself. Then he realised how stupid a question it was. Who wouldn't ask? Ask to go back and save the ones they loved…

'It's… complicated,' said the Doctor, feeling that was one of the worst answers he had ever given. 'But if I kept going back and changing things every time something bad happened, I'd spend my life going round in circles creating dangerous paradoxes and time eddies that would damage… well, everything… eventually.'

'But—' started Ollus.

The Doctor knelt down close to the boy, putting his

hand on his tiny shoulders. 'There are rules, Ollus,' he said. 'Ancient rules. And I have to stick to them.'

Ollus shrugged away and hit the console with all his might. 'But I promised her! I told Jenibeth we'd come back for her!'

'I know,' said the Doctor. 'But it wasn't your promise to make.'

Ollus yelled, 'No!' in unrestrained anger and flew at the Doctor with the clear intention of hitting him. The Doctor closed his eyes, expecting and ready to accept the fierce little blows, but they did not come. He opened his eyes and saw Sabel restraining Ollus, holding his forearms. Ollus twisted and groaned angrily.

'No, Ollus,' Sabel was saying. 'No hitting. Hitting is a bad thing and the Doctor is a good man!'

The Doctor did not feel like a good man at this precise moment in time. At this precise moment, he felt that he should have never responded to the distress call from Alyst and Terrin. Someone else would have eventually rescued the children. He should never have got involved. He must stop doing this, he thought. Stop getting involved in things he could not put right. Things he only ever seemed to make worse.

'But the Daleks will kill Jenibeth,' said Ollus, sobbing, finally letting his arms fall to his sides. Sabel hugged her little brother, enfolding him tightly in her arms, squeezing him, starting to cry herself.

'No,' said the Doctor, suddenly, grasping at a thought. 'They *threatened* to kill her.'

The two children looked at the Doctor, clearly confused.

'*Threatening* and *doing* are not the same thing,' continued the Doctor. An idea was forming in his mind. He wasn't quite sure exactly what the idea was, but it was beginning to grow. 'No, the Daleks love to threaten and they love to take hostages too.'

'What do you mean?' asked Sabel.

'I mean,' said the Doctor. 'There's still a chance for Jenibeth.'

Jenibeth saw the TARDIS disappear from sight, groaning like a great yawning monster, and felt empty inside. She tried to pull herself free from the Dalek sucker stuck to her back. She couldn't. It wouldn't let go.

It hurt.

'Ow!' she complained out loud. But the Dalek still didn't let go.

Another Dalek hovered quickly to where the TARDIS had been, its dome spinning round, its eye stick waving up and down in a rage.

'The Doctor has escaped!' it shouted in its horrible voice.

There was the noise of another Dalek hovering. Jenibeth looked round to see it coming down the stairs. Its eye stick moved to look at her, the blue light in it shining brighter, hurting her eyes to look at it.

'How did you activate the Cradle?' it asked in a voice far less noisy, but just as horrible. 'Answer! Answer! Answer!'

Then Jenibeth remembered what Sabel had said to her in the orphanage back home. Try to think of your favourite thing... jelly blobs. So she did. She imagined she was eating a jelly blob; the juiciest jelly blob there had ever been. She bit into it and the lovely sweet flavour flowed out into her mouth, and for a moment all the scary feelings went away. She looked straight back at the Dalek looking at her… and smiled.

Then suddenly this Dalek looked up.

Jenibeth looked up too. All around her, the sparkling lights that had been filling this big room ever since they had arrived started to go out. After a little while, all the lights had gone, apart from the ones on metal sticks that had been here before.

'Cradle power deactivated!' said another Dalek in a low, grumbling sort of voice.

Jenibeth could hear a deep rumbling sound that made her tummy feel funny. Then she remembered, this noise had been made by the big rocks moving, up in the desert. She thought hard and realised this noise probably meant these rocks were moving back to the way they had been, before all the lights and the fizzy stuff.

'What have you done?' asked the Dalek who had spoken in the less noisy voice.

'I'm having a jelly blob,' Jenibeth answered.

'The child is too undeveloped to comprehend,' said the same Dalek.

Jenibeth thought this sounded funny and smiled back, unable to stop herself giggling a bit.

The Dalek continued. 'But she may yet prove to be a useful hostage. Secure her in a detention cell in the ship.' It moved to face the other Daleks and carried on droning away in its horrible voice.

'Now that we have seen the Cradle power activated, we know for certain that it will serve our purpose. And when the Daleks take control of it, we will activate it again. The Cradle of the Gods will make the Daleks masters of the universe. Masters of the universe! Masters of the universe!'

The other Daleks all started repeating those words, their voices getting higher and higher.

'Masters of the universe! Masters of the universe! Masters of the universe!'

Not even the sweet taste of her imaginary jelly blobs could shut out the terrible noise. It echoed all around the chamber, making her ears buzz painfully. She put her hands flat onto her ears, but it was no good, the horrible noises from the Daleks and their shouting went on and on and on until Jenibeth felt her head would burst.

Chapter Ten
Sunlight Secrets

Lillian Belle stepped into her apartment after another long, hard day reporting news to an ever-dwindling holo-TV audience. Today, she had presented features on drainage facilities and the issue of sun protection for the populations of the four hundred Sunlight Worlds. She had put as much of her heart and soul into it as she could muster, given that she knew that the vast majority of the Sunlight audience would most likely opt to watch one of the hundreds of 'reality' programmes or quizzes.

She gleaned what job satisfaction she could and smiled her tight, restrained smile to her bosses whenever they asked how things were going. She was a fairly big fish in the evaporating pond of current affairs in the world of Sunlight television. She knew that many industry people looked on with a mixture of pity and confusion as she batted away all offers to move over into live 'info-tainment'. They viewed her as a kind of slowly self-destructing crusader in a reality where there was nothing to crusade about any more.

And that was just what she wanted them to think.

Lillian gently closed the front door behind her, took off her light little jacket and hung it on the wall. She breezed gently into her kitchen and made herself a cool, refreshing fruit drink. She then went into her lounge and moved towards the wide, floor-to-ceiling window that looked out onto her small, neat garden area, just big enough for two chairs, a table and a sun shade. A sun shade so vital on a planet constantly soaked in artificial sunlight, courtesy of the Dalek Foundation's life-giving artificial satellites.

As she reached the window, she absently placed a hand against it, letting the warmth of her body temperature mix with the air-conditioned coolness of the plastic glass. Satisfied that she had left her hand there just long enough, she moved back and relaxed onto a sofa.

But her eyes never left that spot on the window where she had rested her hand.

If anyone had been watching her over a period of weeks, they might have noticed that Lillian carried out this little ritual every third day. On the other days, she touched other windows in her apartment, or stroked the lid of her garbage incinerator or brushed her hair against the light fitting in her bedroom. All seemingly pointless little moments in the life of someone entirely unremarkable.

And that was *exactly* what she wanted them to think.

Her eyes still stayed fixed upon the window.

Just a little more time…

Some months back, she had covered one of the few

dramatic events to take place on a Sunlight planet. There had been a train crash. A terrible, freak accident. She had investigated it. She had been told the drivers had survived. But she had never been able to find those drivers or the medics who attended them.

Never one to give up, she had kept on trying to trace them. She had contacted the local government authorities and had been pushed from department to department. She had even attempted contact with the Dalek Foundation itself. All to no avail. But the more she got nowhere, the more she found she wanted to push further. The more she knew that something was really wrong here, because she had always had a strange, uneasy feeling about life here on Sunlight 349.

Then, one day, she had noticed someone looking at her across the street. It was a secret but pointed sort of a look. When she had attempted to cross the street to talk to this person, a skimmer had 'accidentally' got in her way and, when it had cleared, the person had gone.

The next day, she had spotted someone else looking at her. Again, she couldn't quite get to them before they vanished. This time, an automatic streetlight-fixing unit had trundled in front of her.

And the next day, something similar had happened. And the day after that and the day after that... She had started to think she was becoming paranoid or going insane.

Then, one day, Lillian had returned home after a hard day's work at *Sunlight 349 Holo-News* to find a complete stranger sitting in her lounge. He had worn commonplace clothes, dark glasses and had a commonplace kind of face. When she had got close to that face, she had realised there was something... artificial about it.

'This isn't my face,' he had said. 'It's a disguise. You can't see my real face. It's too dangerous.'

'Are you really that ugly?' she had joked.

He had laughed, but it was a brittle, artificial laugh, like bad acting in one of the many 'real-life' dramas on TV.

The man had told her not to push any further on the truth about the train crash.

'Are you something to do with the government?' she had asked.

'We're *nothing* to do with the government,' he had said. 'We are the resistance.' And then he had told her about the adjustments that had been made to her apartment. The technology implanted into the floor-to-ceiling window looking out onto the small garden, the lid of the garbage incinerator, other windows in the house, the light fittings... He had told her what to do and when to do it and what signs to look for when she had done it. This was to be the means of her receiving instructions, she had been told. This was how she could help to bring down the rule of the Daleks.

And then he had injected her with something. Without warning, he had leapt forward and jabbed her with a tiny needle. She had had no time to react or stop him. The effect of it had knocked her unconscious. And then she had fallen ill for about three days. It was like some kind of flu virus. Her bosses had understood. Things were not exactly busy at *Sunlight 349 Holo-News*, she could be spared for a few days.

When she recovered, Lillian remembered what the man had told her and started to touch the windows, the incinerator and the other things in the patterns he had specified. For a long time, nothing had happened.

Then, one day, something did happen. After waiting for five or so minutes, a small yellow mark had appeared on the incinerator lid. As she had been instructed, she touched the mark with her index finger. It had made her feel sick, but it had also given her information. Suddenly, she had known where to look for a clue as to the fate of the freak train-crash drivers.

Three days later, she had managed to find, misfiled in a Medical Department Records Office, a report marked for deletion on the discovery of several bodies from the site of the train crash. The bodies of people who had not died from the effects of the crash, but who had died from massive internal disruption, the result of some form of energy projection, the report had concluded.

She had had no idea what to do with this information; but now at least she knew for certain that something was not right in the Sunlight Worlds. That persistent doubt she had harboured for years, that guilt that had festered because of how grateful her parents had been about it all, her single-minded dedication to finding out the truth, a dedication that had left her cold and alone in her life... Now she knew there really was a justification for it all. It was not just paranoia and depression. And there were other people out there who felt the same way. She was now working for them. Working, in some unfathomable way, to bring the truth to people. It may take time, she thought, but she was part of something important and, most significant of all, something that would reveal the truth about the Dalek Foundation...

Whatever that truth was.

So, as she stared at the window, she expected nothing to happen, just as nothing had happened so many times before. She knew she had to be patient.

Then, a small, deep orange mark appeared on the glass. A thrill of excitement running through her, she got up and calmly placed her finger on the mark. When she withdrew her finger, the mark had gone, but she was already feeling sick and, most importantly, learning something new.

Her mind was starting to receive information from the microscopically minute artificial memory cells in the orange mark. Memory cells programmed to travel straight to her brain.

Her mind was beginning to learn... gradually...

Something...

About...

The Doctor.

When Lillian Belle finally found the Doctor, he was walking around one of Sunlight 349's large, open shopping areas. The central shopping mall, in fact. She saw that he had two children with him. A girl, who was probably about 12 years old, and a boy, who was maybe 5, possibly younger.

Lillian made sure she positioned herself at an angle, across the street, where this Doctor would spot her. But to her frustration, he never seemed to look her way. He simply carried on looking into shop windows at various gigantic holographic TV screens, typical of these shopping malls. Every now and then, he would flick a hand out behind him and wave for the children to follow. For their part, they seemed completely uninterested in the shops and the screens. The Doctor, however, could not keep his eyes off any and every retail outlet and screen within his gaze. This behaviour certainly did not tally with what Lillian knew about the Doctor.

The information she had received talked of a 'known saboteur of Dalek Foundation operations', a 'meddler in the affairs of others' and an 'expert at revolutionary tactics'. At no point did the word 'shopaholic' feature.

Finally, losing patience a little, Lillian moved over to the Doctor's side of the street. As she crossed, she was aware that she would be forgoing the opportunity of dodging behind passing skimmers if the Doctor suddenly turned to look in her direction; but things were getting desperate. The wretched man was simply not behaving as expected.

She saw him gesture for the children to come close to him again as he continued to stare into a window screen, around which a holographic projection of the popular game show *How Nice Is Your Brain?* was showing. Two people were standing opposite each other, with a massive holographic image of their innermost thoughts hanging in the air. A flashing graphic urged viewers to vote on who was the 'nicest contestant' based on what they could see of their memories and thought processes. It was the Sunlight Worlds' top-rated programme.

The children reluctantly slunk up to the Doctor. He was clearly talking to them. Lillian was wondering what he was saying, when she suddenly noticed the small boy standing right in front of her. He had somehow slipped out of her line of sight without her noticing.

'Hello,' said the boy. 'My name is Ollus. I'm with the Doctor, I am.'

Lillian's first instinct was to leave. She made as if to move.

'Don't go,' said Ollus. 'He said you'd try to go, he did. But he's been watching you all the time, you see. In the reflections. So he says there's no point you going, he does.'

Lillian hesitated, confused. Then when she looked back to where the Doctor was, she saw that he was facing her way, waving.

'Busted!' he shouted cheerfully. Then he strode over towards her.

She felt helpless and stupid. What would the resistance people she was working for think of her? Her instructions had been to observe the Doctor and report back. Intrigue him. Let him know he was being watched, but dodge back into the shadows. Subject him to the same initiation she had experienced.

But now, on first contact, here he was, coming straight up to her, hand outstretched.

Lillian looked down at the Doctor's hand and did nothing.

'Well, that's not very friendly,' he said.

'Er...' she started, not really knowing what to say. Lamely, she offered her hand and he shook it heartily.

'There, that's better, isn't it?' said the Doctor, beaming at her. 'So let's start with your name and then we can move on to why you're stalking me. Don't worry, I'm not cross, just, you know, a bit intrigued. Well, who wouldn't be, eh?' He gave a little laugh. She found she could not respond.

'Oh dear,' continued the Doctor. 'Not very happy today, are we? What's the matter? Have I spoiled everything? Sorry, I tend to do that, but the fact is that I'm not in the mood for pussyfooting around because I'm after some answers! Got any of those, er... what did you say your name was? Oh, that's right, you didn't.'

Much to her own annoyance, Lillian just stared. The Doctor stared back, still holding her hand. She averted her eyes from his almost mesmerising gaze and pulled her hand away, but then she just saw the children, who were also staring at her.

'We need to rescue our sister,' said the girl. 'So we can't hang around.'

This was all getting far more complicated than Lillian had expected.

'Lillian,' she finally said. 'Lillian Belle.'

'Well, ding-dong, hello Miss Belle!' said the Doctor, grabbing her hand again and forcing her to shake his. 'So, me and my friends Sabel and Ollus here have just done a round trip of ten randomly selected Sunlight Worlds, just to get a flavour of what the Daleks are up to.'

Lillian looked around sharply, to see if anyone was watching. Luckily, it seemed as though everyone in the street was quite happily getting on with their own business.

'Making you nervous, am I, Lillian?' asked the Doctor, earnestly. 'That seems odd to me. I mean, I've been to plenty of planets run by the Daleks and they're usually pretty dreary places, full of slave labour camps and zombified Robomen shouting orders and hitting people. And what do I find on the Sunlight Worlds? Nothing much wrong! Imagine that! Eh?'

'Look...' Lillian started.

'Look? I *have* been looking,' continued the Doctor, fearlessly. 'I grant you, it's all a bit "new town", bit Milton Keynes, but to be honest, it's all pretty... *nice*. *Nice* places for *nice* people to live in relatively comfortable surroundings... *nicely*. Holographic TV everywhere packed with quizzes and reality shows, a thriving, free press that no one takes much notice of – but then why should they, when everything's so...' he swallowed hard and unpleasantly, evidently unhappy with what he was about to say, 'lovely and *nice*?'

Lillian withdrew her hand again, but placed it on the Doctor's shoulder.

'You should come with me,' she said quietly and urgently, close to his ear.

The Doctor turned sharply to her and spoke equally quietly and urgently. 'You see, I'm just running out of patience, Lillian Belle. I want to know why the Daleks are covering up their true nature so skilfully. I want to know what they're up to. And most of all, I want to let everyone know the truth about the Daleks and their long, apparently forgotten history of conquest and extermination. Any ideas how I might do that?'

*

Deep inside a gigantic spacecraft, at the centre of a structure fashioned over centuries so that it could actually protrude into the Time Vortex itself, the Dalek Time Controller was observing events. Behind it, a squad of high-ranking Daleks assembled. Chief among them was the Dalek Supreme in its pristine white, formidable, bulky armour casing.

Twitching impatiently on the spot, the Supreme dared to speak. 'We should intervene now!'

Its words echoed around the time chamber and spiralled out into the Vortex, evaporating into nothing.

The silence was ominous. The other Daleks edged back, instinctively nervous.

Then, the Dalek Time Controller spoke. Its voice purred quietly, hardly vocalised at all.

'No,' it said.

The Dalek Supreme was not used to being contradicted. 'We must proceed to activate the Cradle of the Gods and—'

'No!' the Time Controller suddenly screeched. The Supreme edged backwards at this.

The Time Controller continued, quietly now. 'An infinite number of factors must be taken into account. The Doctor's course is set. Set by *me*.'

For the first time in a long while, the Dalek Time Controller turned away from the Vortex and faced the other Daleks. The swirling, blurring rings across its grating increased their rotation as if in excitement. The other Daleks swayed, almost mesmerised by this motion.

'We must not intervene. Any intervention now

would create disturbances in the flow of time that would ultimately harm the Daleks,' it said. 'This is my purpose. That which I have been engineered for... the ultimate victory of the Daleks through pure strategy.'

Then the Dalek Time Controller suddenly shot forwards, moving so that it was almost touching the Dalek Supreme. The Controller's words were almost inaudible, but the power of them was devastating.

'And...

'You...

'Will...

'Obey.'

The Dalek Supreme stared back at the Controller's blue, glaring eye lens and uttered two words it was not accustomed to saying.

'I... obey.'

When the Doctor, Sabel and Ollus arrived with Lillian Belle at her apartment, it didn't take the Doctor long to spot the incredible technology that had been installed here. He immediately bombarded Lillian with questions. He found out that she was a journalist, that she was suspicious about the Daleks. She told him how she had discovered that the drivers from the train crash had probably been killed by Daleks. She told him everything she knew about the secret resistance who, like her, knew that the Daleks were planning something. Something terrible.

For the first time, the Doctor noticed that Sabel was joining in with Ollus in his toy spaceship adventures. She was looking after Ollus, the Doctor realised. She was taking on the role of parent, very probably mimicking things she had heard her late mother and father say. The tragedy she had experienced was forcing her to grow up faster.

After glancing affectionately at the children, the Doctor turned his attention back to Lillian. He saw her looking warmly at Sabel and Ollus.

'How did they lose their sister?' Lillian asked quietly.

'The Daleks took her,' said the Doctor. 'But we're going to get her back.'

'How can you be so sure?'

'I have to be. She's alive. She has to be. It's my number one objective, and nobody gets in the way of my number one objective – not even the Daleks.'

The Doctor sprang off the sofa he had been reclining on and moved close to the large window overlooking the small garden.

'So,' he said. 'Fascinating memory-cell technology. Very advanced. Very advanced for a small resistance group working undercover and doing so little to topple the rule of the Daleks.'

'How do you topple an occupying force that everyone trusts?' asked Lillian pointedly.

'Fair point,' the Doctor conceded. 'Fair point. Still… does seem rather over-elaborate to me.'

'It has to be,' said Lillian. 'We can't risk anyone finding out.'

'And yet *you* gave yourself away pretty easily,' the Doctor snapped back at her, raising an admonishing finger.

Lillian seemed a little stung and couldn't think of

185

anything to say. She looked ashamed.

The Doctor breezed on. 'So, what happens now? I'll tell you what happens now. You take me to these underground resistance people. I want to meet them. I want to help them. I want to find out what the Daleks are up to. Well, actually, I know what they're up to, they want to get their protruberances on the Cradle of the Gods.'

'The Cradle—' Lillian started to ask.

'But,' the Doctor ploughed straight on, 'I want to find out what these Sunlight Worlds have got to do with it all. How could four hundred nice, nice, *nice* little worlds for *nice* people to live on feature in a plan to harness some kind of ancient, destructive force?'

'I...' began Lillian. 'I didn't know... Is that what they're doing?'

'Oh, they're always doing things like this,' the Doctor said, peering more closely at the window and the remnants of the faded, orange blob. 'Activating weapons, invading planets, trying to destroy everything for no apparent reason...' His nose touched the window. 'My job is to stop them.'

'No!' called out Lillian in alarm. 'The resistance will know you've touched it!'

Sabel and Ollus stopped playing, looking over at the Doctor worriedly.

The Doctor staggered back from the window, rubbing his stomach.

'Yes, does make you feel a little unsettled in the tummy, doesn't it?' he said, managing a smile to the children. The nausea passed. 'Interesting,' he continued.

His mind was flooding with ideas... all about him. 'Very interesting.'

In his mind's eye, he could see an image of himself and the children on Gethria. An image of himself in court on Carthedia. Then he was running with the children away from the orphanage, heading to escape in the skimmer.

'Your resistance people seem remarkably well informed,' he said.

'They have someone inside the government offices,' Lillian explained. 'They're able to tap into top-secret Dalek files.'

'I see,' said the Doctor, moving closer and closer to her and staring right into her eyes. 'I see, I see, I see... So! How do we get to see them?'

'You don't,' said Lillian. 'They get to see you.'

Chapter Eleven

The Resistance

Ollus wanted his sister Jenibeth back.

It hurt so much inside. But he couldn't help thinking back to when he had shouted out. He could see her, surrounded by the Daleks on Gethria. He could hear his words, calling out to her, promising that they would come back for her.

When he thought of this, it made him screw up his face and make a moaning sound.

Sabel would see this and put her arm around him or give him a little kiss or say, 'Do you want to play spaceships?'

He knew she didn't really like playing spaceships, but it was Sabel's way of making him feel better, and he was glad of it.

He loved his little spaceship toy. He remembered the day his Daddy had given it to him.

'You take good care of that, Ollus.'

He would. It was all that he had left of his Daddy.

He was playing with it now, as he ran along the

streets of this Sunlight World. It was the kind of thing that his Mummy and Daddy used to tell him not to do back home on Carthedia.

'Don't run on the pavements,' they would say. 'It's dangerous.'

But now that the Doctor was looking after them, it was OK to run along the pavements. In fact, the Doctor had told him to run around as much as he liked, make lots of noise and enjoy himself… On the pavements… In the shops… Anywhere they went on this planet.

And they had certainly been to a lot of places. Every day for really quite a long time. He couldn't remember how long. They had been to lots of places. And all of them looked the same. The same streets, the same shops, the same skimmer cars hovering around.

The Doctor and Sabel would walk around, chatting, and Ollus would run around and play, all day.

There was only one special thing he had to do in return. Just like he'd done when Lillian had been watching the Doctor. He had to watch out for people who were watching the Doctor, and if he found someone watching the Doctor, someone who had dark glasses and a funny sort of face, he was to go up to them and distract them, so that the Doctor could sneak up on them and surprise them, just as he had done with Lillian.

Lillian was at work, being a journalist, so she wasn't with them this time.

So far, over all the days of playing around in the streets and bumping into people and being told off by strangers for treading on their feet, Ollus hadn't seen a single person really watching the Doctor the way Lillian had done.

Then the day finally came when Ollus spotted someone. A man in a plain, dark coat with the hood pulled up, and wearing plain, dark trousers. He was also wearing dark glasses and he had been standing, watching the Doctor from across the street for a long, long time – much longer than people normally watched. Ollus was sure that this was it.

Time for him to distract the man.

'Do you want to play with me and my spaceship?' Ollus asked the man.

'Go away,' the man had said. But Ollus knew he must keep on trying. And he did. He tried and tried and tried, jumping up and down in front of the man until the man seemed to get quite cross.

But just when he did get cross and started to shout, the Doctor was suddenly standing in front of the man. He had sneaked round while Ollus had been doing his distracting job.

'Hello!' the Doctor said to the man. The Doctor had a big smile on his face. 'You took your time. No point running away now, I've spotted you. Right, come on. Take me to your leader.'

The Doctor carried Ollus and held Sabel close to him as the man from the resistance, who had been shamefully flushed out by a 4-year-old, ushered them down some steps into what seemed to be a disused underground train terminus. It was dark, with damp walls dripping, and a few, widely spaced electric lamps which flickered and buzzed, emitting a pale, yellowish light. The air smelt dead and musty. Rusting train tracks led off into the darkness. Battered and abandoned carriages glimmered in the half-light like fading fragments of history.

'This a secret rendezvous place, then?' asked the Doctor in hushed tones. 'The unmentioned underbelly of Sunlight 349, eh?' He was rather excited at this. He felt as though he was in some kind of spy novel. Despite the seriousness of the threat from the Daleks, he couldn't help feeling there was something a little self-consciously 'cloak and dagger' about this resistance business. As they reached the bottom of the steps, he moved round across the grimy platform area, still holding on to Ollus tightly and pulling Sabel with him. He was trying to manoeuvre to get another look at this resistance man's face.

Lillian had been right. There was something odd about it, if indeed this was the same man. Was it a disguise? He wasn't sure. At first glance, it had looked like a normal face. But the Doctor had got a brief, closer look... and it was...

Odd.

'Hope you don't mind my asking,' ventured the Doctor. 'But what exactly have you done to disguise your face?'

'It is no concern of yours,' said the man, keeping in the shadows. 'You cannot know any of our true identities. It's safer that way.'

'You mean, if the Daleks catch me, I won't be able to give you away?' asked the Doctor.

'Exactly,' said the man.

'Oh, believe you me,' said the Doctor. 'If the Daleks capture me, they won't give tuppence about who you are or what you're up to. I'm their biggest problem. But you know that, don't you? Because you're remarkably well informed, so I gather, from your ingenious memory-cell technology. You seem to know as much about me as the Daleks do.'

At that moment, other figures emerged from the darkness, some way off, walking up the tracks. Ollus noticed them first, poking the Doctor rather painfully in the ear to get his attention. Sabel retreated, pressing against his tweed jacket.

'It's all right, it's all right,' breathed the Doctor to the children in his best, reassuring voice. He didn't really believe that, but he hoped they would.

'I need a wee,' whispered Ollus.

'Well… can you just hold on for a little while?' asked the Doctor, rather desperately.

'He probably can't,' said Sabel, in a very sensible, grown-up sort of voice. Ollus nodded in agreement.

'Well, hello!' the Doctor said aloud to the approaching figures. They were all dressed similarly to the first resistance man. There were four of them, three of them women. 'I know this rather punctures the drama of the moment, but I have a toilet emergency with my youngest friend here.'

The four figures stepped up onto the platform and joined the first resistance man.

'Just… just go and sort Ollus out back there,' whispered the Doctor, pointing back to a corridor leading off the stairs whilst lowering Ollus down and putting the boy's hand in Sabel's.

Sabel obediently took Ollus away with her, heading in the direction of something that looked like an old, broken storm drain.

'Sorry about this,' said the Doctor, with a slightly guilty, apologetic grin. 'Anyway, I'm the Doctor – you probably know that – who are you?'

'No names,' said one of the women in a rather flat voice.

'Oh. All right, then,' said the Doctor, making sure he fully displayed his disappointment. 'So, what do we do now? Devise a secret plan to topple the Daleks? Plan a raid on a flying saucer? Who's going to wear the Roboman disguise? Do the Daleks even have Robomen here? So many questions, aren't there?'

He ran out of steam. The assembled resistance people merely stood and looked at him.

'What do you know of the Dalek plan?' one of the other women asked blankly.

'You go first,' said the Doctor. 'You've been here longer than me.'

'*We're* asking the questions,' said the first man, somewhat aggressively. He stepped forward, as if to threaten.

'Oh, there's not going to be violence, is there?' asked the Doctor. 'Because I hate violence. That's the sort of thing the Daleks like.' The Doctor took a step or two towards the man, hoping to get a better look at the oddness of his face. 'And we're here to defeat them, aren't we?' he added, pointedly.

At that moment, Sabel made a 'Psssst!' noise from

behind the Doctor. Slightly irritated, the Doctor smiled politely at the resistance man, then called back as quietly as he could to Sabel and Ollus.

'Look, just get on with whatever it is you're doing and hurry back.'

'No, it's serious,' whispered Sabel harshly.

'*What?*' said the Doctor, getting properly irritated now. Then he huffed and shrugged his shoulders. 'Sorry, hang on a minute.'

The Doctor walked back to where Sabel and Ollus were, just to the left of the steps. To his relief, it seemed that Ollus had already taken care of his lavatorial needs. But the little boy seemed very agitated. He was pointing past the stairs, down a pale, flickering corridor.

The Doctor knew something was genuinely the matter, so he whispered, 'What is it, Ollus?'

Ollus almost silently mouthed the words, 'I heard Daleks moving, I did. Down there.'

The Doctor paused, listening.

'What are you doing?' demanded the resistance man, approaching.

'Ssssh!' ssshed the Doctor. But the man kept walking. Then, sure enough, even over the echoing click of the approaching footsteps, the Doctor could hear a faint whine of Dalek traction and the distant purr of a rotating dome section.

'We've been followed,' said the Doctor, urgently to the man.

'What?' he asked.

'Daleks!' the Doctor said. 'We've got to get out of here.'

'Look!' shouted Sabel. She was pointing into the darkness beyond the tracks, where the other four resistance people had come from.

Everyone turned to look into the darkness. Except that it wasn't dark. Now there were twenty or more hovering blue lights flitting around, getting bigger and bigger.

'Dalek eyes!' shouted the Doctor. And at that moment, the dim light of the station partially revealed that these blue lights were glowing lenses atop the forms of twenty emerging Daleks, hovering over the train tracks.

As he shouted, 'Run!' he noticed, too, that Daleks were starting to glide down the corridor where Ollus had heard them. 'It's a raid!'

The Doctor grabbed Ollus and Sabel and dragged them up the steps. 'Thank goodness for your tiny bladder,' whispered the Doctor hoarsely – then he tripped and lost his grip on Ollus. As the little boy tumbled, his toy spaceship bounced out of his pocket and clattered down the steps.

'Leave it, Ollus!' shouted Sabel. But it was too late. Recovering, her brother was already running down after his precious toy.

Meanwhile, the resistance people were fleeing for their lives. Two of them tried to hide in the derelict train carriages, but it was no use. The Daleks spotted them. Three units peeled off from the main formation and aimed their weapons squarely at the carriages.

'Exterminate!' one of them screeched triumphantly.

Pure energy leapt from their metal gun attachments,

crashing into the carriages, which immediately burst into an inferno of blue, writhing light. The roaring sound of impact was deafening in this confined, underground space.

Just as Ollus's little hands grasped his skittering toy, the Doctor managed to grab Ollus and start to haul him back up the stairs.

'Keep going, Sabel!' cried the Doctor, heaving Ollus onto his back. Sabel, who had been hesitating near the top of the steps, turned and ran up as fast as she could. The Doctor glanced back, just in time to catch sight of the three other resistance fighters being cut down by Dalek fire. In the dim light, he could not see the blasted, photo-negative image of their demise – they simply seemed to burst into flames like figures on a strangely bluish bonfire.

Emerging quickly into the daylight above, the Doctor and Ollus shielded their eyes from the sudden change in light temperature. Sabel, already acclimatising, grabbed the Doctor's hand, dragging him along the street. But the Doctor turned and secured the door to the stairs behind them. It crashed shut with an enormous clang.

'Will that stop them?' asked Sabel, panting a little.

'No… But I think this will,' he said, pointing all around. They all looked at the pastel-shaded suburban idyll that was Sunlight 349. Calm-looking buildings, large holographic screens at regular intervals featuring quizzes and reality shows… 'They've got people here believing they're living the good life. Chasing fugitives down the street, all guns blazing doesn't quite fit.'

The Doctor lowered Ollus gently down to the

pavement. This had been a quiet area when they had first been led here by the now deceased resistance man, and it was indeed still fairly empty, but there were the odd skimmers still passing by. Further up the street, a group of children were being led along by some adults. Some kind of school outing, perhaps.

'They… the Daleks… killed all those…' stammered Sabel, clearly in shock.

'I know, I know,' said the Doctor, putting his hand on her shoulder. 'Seems that the Daleks are still prepared to revert to their old ways beyond the public gaze.' He smoothed down his jacket and straightened his hair. 'Come on. We've got to find Lillian.'

'She's at work, journalisting,' said Ollus.

'I know,' said the Doctor. 'Come on.'

Chapter Twelve
Start the Revolution

'The frequency of skimmer bus services on the orbital route in City Zone 004 has come under criticism again, during the latest local council meeting. Those living on the outer ring of the zone have made representations to the council, making the case that with the population rising—'

Lillian Belle was in mid-flow, recording a piece to holo-vid camera when the door of her personal studio burst open and the Doctor entered with Sabel and Ollus.

'Sorry!' announced the Doctor cheerily, shutting the door behind them. 'Not interrupting anything important, are we? No, I thought not.'

He leant over and switched off the camera.

Lillian was furious that he had intruded upon her work. 'How the hell did you get in here?' she asked.

'Ooh, I have my methods,' said the Doctor, waving a strange wallet, snapping it shut and popping it in his inside jacket pocket. She hadn't the slightest idea what he meant.

'What I'm more concerned with,' continued the Doctor, 'is how to let the population of the Sunlight Worlds know that they're being governed for some nefarious purpose by the most evil creatures in the known universe. Any ideas spring to mind? Hmm? Given that you work in a *news TV station*?'

'What exactly are you suggesting?' asked Lillian, taken aback, fearing the worst.

'I'm suggesting you put me on the telly,' said the Doctor. He switched on her camera again and angled it towards himself, swivelling so that he could also see himself in the holo-display pad she had next to her. 'What's the matter? Don't you think I'm holo-genic?' He wiggled his chin and stroked it.

Lillian had found the Doctor exasperating almost from the moment she had met him. But now he was surpassing himself.

'Doctor,' she said in hushed tones, trying to indicate to him to keep his voice down. 'The resistance—'

'The Daleks shot them,' said little Ollus.

'Shot?' Lillian felt a coldness inside her. 'But...'

'But nothing,' said the Doctor. 'We were there. We saw it.'

'We met them underground, down some steps,' explained Sabel. 'There were five of them—'

'Only five?' asked Lillian.

'All dressed the same, with funny faces and dark glasses,' said Sabel.

'Then the Daleks shot them,' added Ollus.

'Yes, I think she got that bit,' said the Doctor. '*Shot*, as in, *just like those poor train drivers*. You remember them? You remember, the reason you got involved with the resistance in the first place? Well, it's time to step up to the plate, Lillian. I'm sure there are more than five resistance people out there, but clearly the Daleks are aware of them and willing to cut them down the moment they get too bold. Perhaps the moment *you* get too bold. So, before the Daleks come for you… What do you say? Wanna start a revolution?'

'I…' she started to say, but then her words froze inside her. Her thoughts were tumbling. She felt like her stomach was in free fall. All those paranoid feelings were being dragged into the cold light of day. Everything her parents had loved and been grateful for was going to be exposed as a terrible, cruel and ruthless lie.

'I do,' she said, realising in those words how true they were. 'I do want to start a revolution. But how…?'

'Don't worry,' said the Doctor.

Lillian couldn't think of one reason why she shouldn't worry.

'I've got a plan,' the Doctor told her.

Two hours later, and the Doctor, Sabel and Ollus were in the central shopping mall of City Zone 004. This was the place where Lillian had first spotted the Doctor, where the Doctor had first come to fathom out what the Daleks were up to. He had taken Sabel and Ollus on a whistle-stop tour of the Sunlight Worlds. They had seen on the scanner in the TARDIS that there were four hundred planets, all surrounded by artificial satellites. Some maintained gravity, some gave artificial sunlight. All of them, the Doctor pointed out, sustained life on a group of planets that would otherwise have been lifeless and uninhabitable. But, for some reason, the Daleks were expending vast amounts of energy on sustaining these planets. The Doctor had asked why then, and he was still no closer to getting an answer.

What he *was* closer to, however, was fixing the channel setting of a holographic TV screen in this shopping mall. Sabel was once again indulging Ollus by playing spaceships with him. The Doctor paused for a moment, not for the first time admiring the resilience of these children, but worrying about the deep trauma that lay beneath the surface. That was the tragedy of the Daleks. They not only caused horrific catastrophes on a planetary scale, their actions burned right down into the personal lives of their victims.

He resumed his work on the screen. No one had seemed too bothered that he was waving his sonic screwdriver around it, although he did, at one point, have to present his psychic paper to a lone security patrol officer in order to prove that he was an 'official maintenance operative'.

'That's it,' said the Doctor, clicking the sonic screwdriver off and relaxing on a bench in front of the screen.

'What's it?' asked Sabel, looking up from her game with Ollus, who was now clambering onto her back, yelling, 'Stand by for landing!' with holograms fizzing wildly from his toy.

'I've managed to route all holographic screens throughout Sunlight 349 through this screen's channel controls,' said the Doctor proudly.

'What about the other planets?' asked Ollus, sliding off Sabel's back and coming in to land on the pavement. 'Ow,' he added, as he bumped his nose.

'Once this world is in uproar about the truth,' said the Doctor, 'I imagine it won't take long for the news to spread.'

He wondered for a moment whether he had the right to destroy the peace and calm here. As far as he could tell, this whole generation of people who had lived under the benevolence of the Daleks was not really suffering in any way. There were no slave camps, no executions, no oppressive rules. Occasionally, it seemed, the Daleks would let their true natures show and someone would be killed, and that would be hushed up. But were the numbers of those killed really any higher than the murder rates in so-called civilised worlds? He doubted it.

Here he was again, though... Interfering. Making judgements about people's lives. Doing the very thing he had vowed never to do again. Maybe he should just let this generation of humans sort out their problems for themselves...

But then, he thought about the Cradle of the Gods. The awesome power to create or destroy planets. How that part of the Dalek plan fitted in with these worlds, he had no idea. But he was certain the Cradle could only be a force for destruction. It must be, he thought. Why else would the Daleks want it so badly? And if the Daleks were intent on unleashing such a force, then he had no choice but to stop them.

He was distracted from his thoughts by Lillian, running across the street to them.

'It's set, it's ready,' she said, breathlessly. 'It will go live in about thirty seconds.' She had clearly run all the way from the *Sunlight 349 Holo-News* building. 'What have you been doing here? How are you going to make sure that everyone—'

The Doctor smiled and clicked a control on his sonic screwdriver. It emitted a truncated buzz. Then the Doctor gestured all around.

Every single screen around him had suddenly changed to display the large white circle and blue lettering of the *Sunlight 349 Holo-News* channel logo. Lillian gasped in awe.

'I know,' said the Doctor, beaming. 'Clever. And that's what everyone on this planet is seeing.'

'No… not just that,' said Lillian.

'Oh,' said the Doctor, a little crestfallen. 'What?'

'It's the first time I've ever seen our channel on any of these screens,' she said. 'It's usually all the game show and quiz stuff. No one wants to watch the news when they're shopping. Huh… no one wants to watch the news at all.'

Suddenly, the picture changed, and the Doctor's face filled all the screens in the mall. His image seemed to hesitate for a moment.

'Is it working?' the Doctor on the screen asked, his voice booming out all over the shopping mall. Ollus laughed. Sabel ssshed him.

'This is serious,' she whispered, loudly.

The real Doctor spun round to clock people's reactions in the mall. He knew that this image was now playing on every holographic screen throughout the planet. They were on the brink of global meltdown.

'I'm going to get the sack, aren't I?' ventured Lillian.

'Oh, I'd say that'll be the least of your worries,' said the Doctor, feeling a keen sense of anticipation.

'Right, then,' said the Doctor on the screen. 'Here is a special announcement for everyone on Sunlight 349…'

The people walking around the shopping centre were starting to stop and take notice.

'The Daleks are the most evil creatures in the known universe,' said the Doctor on the screen. He waited for the impact to sink in.

The real Doctor waited for the reaction. A couple of the people in a small, gathering crowd looked at him and then back at the screen, then back again.

'Yep,' said the Doctor with a smile. 'That's me all right.'

'They are ruling this planet and all the Sunlight Worlds for some terrible, unknown purpose,' continued the Doctor on the screen.

Then the crowd started to chuckle.

'No, wait,' said the real Doctor. 'It's not a joke.'

But the chuckling continued.

'Now, I know the Daleks have transformed your lives,' the Doctor on the screen was saying, 'that they've saved many of you from poverty and starvation…'

The chuckling stopped as the growing crowds settled down, agreeing with this.

'But they're not doing this for you,' said the screen Doctor. 'They're doing it for themselves, because they have a weapon that they're going to use to destroy planets.'

A few scoffing noises came from the crowd, and minor outbursts of laughter started up.

'Why are you laughing?' asked the real Doctor. He turned to Lillian. 'Why are they laughing?'

The Doctor on the screen continued, his expression strong with the certainty that he was about to start a revolution. 'Today, I saw five people killed. And for what? For daring to question the authority of the Daleks!'

The people in the crowd started to scoff now. Some were openly hurling abuse.

'And I have no doubt that unless we all band together to take action, many more people will be killed by the Daleks,' said the screen Doctor. 'So I urge you. Stand with me and—'

One of the crowd members had stepped forward, jabbed at an on-screen control and changed the channel. The crowd let out a huge cheer of approval as the latest edition of *How Nice Is Your Brain?* started. A high-energy theme tune with a bewilderingly fast bass line and a cloying, chiming melody of tinkling bells and bizarrely ascending strings rang out to the delight of the crowd.

'I'm Mathias Sunam!' said a brightly dressed man with a frighteningly insincere, fixed smile and sweat on his top lip. His face was on every screen in the mall. 'And I'll be your host for the latest, nerve-melting edition of *How Nice Is Your Brain?'*

The Doctor felt utterly defeated. He turned to Lillian.

'Did that really just happen?' he asked her.

She nodded slowly.

Chapter Thirteen
Dalek Litigator

Sabel and Ollus were staring up at the screens, enraptured by what they saw. The first contestants were already stepping up to the podium on the holographic TV show *How Nice Is Your Brain?*

The Doctor looked away from them and up into the sky, in despair. Was there nothing that could be done for this Dalek generation? Were they so beguiled by the petty pleasures of the Sunlight Worlds that nothing could make them realise the terrible danger they were in?

Lillian walked close to the Doctor and put a hand on his shoulder.

'This... this is how *I* felt,' she said. 'Looks like I'll have lost my job for nothing.'

'Oh no,' said the Doctor.

'How would you know?' she asked.

'No,' said the Doctor. 'I meant, "oh no" as in, look up there!'

He pointed right up into the sky. A small, glowing

dot was descending towards them. As they watched, the artificial sunlight glinted off it, revealing as it got closer that it was a metallic, disc-shaped object. An object all too familiar to the Doctor.

'A Dalek ship!' he shouted at the top of his voice, in warning. But he was drowned out by a game show that had its audience in the palm of its glossy, bejewelled hand.

'Are you sure it's a Dalek ship?' asked Lillian.

'Of course I'm sure! I've spent all my lives fighting the Daleks, I know a Dalek ship when I see one!' screamed the Doctor in frustration over more jangling music from the screens.

Lillian moved close to the Doctor, speaking right into his ear. Her voice was trembling. 'What... what do you think they're going to do?'

'Do? Oh, probably offer us all tickets to see *How Nice is Your Brain?* or something,' sneered the Doctor. 'No, don't you see?' he asked. 'I've gone and done it now. The people here may not believe me. There may not be an uprising in progress, but I've gone and done it and prodded the hornet's nest.'

'You mean... they're going to attack?' asked Lillian, her eyes widening. 'They're going to kill us, like they killed those resistance people and the train drivers?'

The Doctor turned resolutely to the crowd and brandished his sonic screwdriver.

'Listen to me!' he cried out to them.

But they were simply not interested.

'Right,' he said and activated the sonic screwdriver, switching off all the screens. There was a massed groan, like this was an inflatable crowd that had suddenly been punctured. But then, bit by bit, random cries of abuse started to fly the Doctor's way.

'That's better,' said the Doctor, climbing on top of a bench, so that he could be seen by the maximum number of people. 'Now I've really got your attention!'

'Go back to wherever you came from, you nutter!' an old man hollered out at him.

'Yes, thanks for that,' smiled the Doctor. 'But if you want to stay alive long enough to insult me again, you'd better LISTEN!'

For a moment, the crowd was stunned into silence by the fierceness of the Doctor's voice. He drew breath to speak again. Already he could hear the silence dissolving into mutters, but he persisted.

'You may not believe what I had to say on the screen, but it's too late now.'

Behind him, he could hear the sound of the Dalek saucer descending. Its anti-grav engines were now preparing for touchdown.

'The Daleks are coming!' yelled the Doctor. 'Run! Run for your lives!'

The crowd stared back at him, the mumbling and muttering gained momentum. Someone wandered over to the main screen and touched a number of controls. Suddenly all the screens were back on and the contestants on *How Nice Is Your Brain?* were on their podiums, smiling nervously. A huge round of applause ignited in the crowd. It was so loud, it almost drowned out the sound of the saucer landing.

The Doctor ran his hand through his hair and shook

his head. He looked down to see Sabel and Ollus, still staring up at the screen, caught up in it all, clapping their hands together along with everyone else. He turned to see the saucer complete its landing, having skilfully manoeuvred itself into the limited space available. The anti-grav motors powered down with a deep, vibrating hum.

'Should we... should we run for it?' asked Lillian tentatively.

The Doctor stared at the saucer. A hatchway was already opening and a ramp was sliding down. People in the crowd were starting to turn and look at it. Some pointed and smiled, others carried on their applause, directing it at the Dalek ship now.

Some cheering started.

Cheering... for the Daleks?

'I don't know,' said the Doctor, feeling sick inside. 'I feel like my whole universe has been turned upside down.'

Then he looked down at the children. Whatever happened, he knew he must protect them.

'Sabel, Ollus!' he called. They reluctantly looked up at him as he jumped down and took their hands. 'Stay close,' he said. The children tutted, irritated that they had been taken away from their entertainment.

Bronze-armoured Daleks were now filing down the ramp from the saucer. The Doctor stared hard at them. If he, Lillian and the children ran from them now, the Daleks could easily cut them down.

As four of the Daleks reached the bottom of the ramp, one of them continued its advance, whilst the three others fanned out, crabbing sideways, quickly and efficiently positioning themselves near the exits of the shopping mall, eyestalks fixing on the Doctor.

'That's it, then,' the Doctor murmured. 'Trapped.'

The Dalek advancing towards him was very close now. The crowd's applause for it and the other Daleks was getting louder. Someone had turned the sound down on the holographic TV screens. They were now all enraptured by the Daleks.

'Oh, just stop it, will you?' yelled the Doctor, the anger in him surging to the surface.

Stunned by this latest outburst from the Doctor, the crowd's applause and cheering dissolved into a smattering of single claps and muted chatter. The Dalek, too, stopped, almost as if it had been commanded by the Doctor.

He stared at this Dalek. He knew he had seen this particular Dalek before. Once again, he could see the strange blurring effect in the middle of its upper grating section. And now there was a sharp, stinging pain in his head. He winced.

'Are any of you seeing this too?' he murmured to Sabel, Ollus and Lillian.

'Seeing what?' asked Lillian, clearly bewildered. Sabel and Ollus looked confused.

'A sort of blur in the middle of that Dalek...' but even as the Doctor uttered the words, he knew they could not see it. 'Just me, then. So, Mr Dalek Litigator, what brings *you* here?' he asked. 'Oh yes, I recognised you, you see.'

'You are illegally holding these children,' the Litigator stated, firmly and precisely. The blur in its grating seemed to have completely vanished now, and the pain was fading slowly.

The crowd started to mutter disapprovingly. Some people shouted out 'Shame!' and 'Shouldn't be allowed' and other, more extreme comments.

'You hypocrite!' shouted the Doctor, slightly ashamed that his anger at the Daleks was probably making him look like a crazy person who just shouted a lot. 'You're "illegally" holding their sister.'

'You will present proof of this unfounded allegation,' the Dalek Litigator purred in what the Doctor felt for a moment were distinctly non-Dalek-like tones.

Ollus immediately blurted out, 'We saw you take her! On Gethria! You took my sister!'

Ollus's words rang out around the mall and the crowd fell utterly silent again. The Doctor patted Ollus on the shoulder and gently ssshed him, feeling some pride at the little boy's bravery.

'This child's evidence is inadmissible,' said the Litigator.

'Why?' demanded Sabel. 'I was there too! We saw you take Jenibeth!'

'You have both been influenced by the Doctor, who is known to be... *unreliable*,' the Dalek Litigator said, focusing on Ollus, Sabel and then the Doctor in turn.

'So what are you going to do?' challenged the Doctor. 'Exterminate us all?'

The crowd became tangibly uneasy.

'Interesting, isn't it?' said the Doctor. 'They all apparently trust you Daleks. They even applaud you. They're grateful to you for having saved them from galactic economic meltdown... But there's still something, isn't there?'

The Doctor moved away from Ollus, Sabel and Lillian and walked straight up to the Litigator. He prodded its casing. 'Still something about a Dalek that a human being can't quite trust.'

'Silence!' the Litigator barked.

A murmuring ripple went through the crowd. Ollus and Sabel cringed in fear and Lillian immediately stepped forward to comfort them. They clasped her, urgently.

The Doctor was grinning, showing some satisfaction to his old foes. He looked around at the Daleks covering the exits. He could see that they had become twitchy. Their gunsticks flicked from potential target to potential target, covering the area in case of an emergency. But their aim always returned to the Doctor.

'Showing your true colours, are you?' the Doctor taunted. 'Who was it said a leopard can never change its spots? They were right, weren't they? So go on, then...'

His voice descended to a whisper.

'Exterminate me.'

The Litigator remained stock still. Its fiercely cold blue lens light constant in its penetrating stare.

'Oh, you're good,' said the Doctor, daring to pat the Dalek's dome section. 'You're very good. Yes, you don't do that sort of thing any more, do you? Eh?' Then he added, mockingly, 'You spend all your time making lovely *nice* planets for *nice* people to live on now, don't you?'

'These children are wards of the state of Carthedia.

They must be returned there,' said the Litigator.

The Doctor made sure he spoke aloud now, for the sake of the crowd. Although they were set against him, they were his only tangible defence now. If the Daleks wanted so badly to maintain their illusion of civilised behaviour, for whatever secret reason, then the Doctor had to make sure the crowd stayed interested. If he was right, the Daleks wouldn't dare to do anything to tarnish their image in front of the people of Sunlight 349.

'These children are orphans!' he shouted. 'Orphaned by the Daleks. There's nothing left for them on Carthedia except a life in some appalling institution, because *you* seized their family's assets.'

'Because you have committed hate crimes against the Dalek Foundation,' countered the Litigator.

'Hate crimes?' mocked the Doctor. 'Oh, do me a favour. You're the experts when it comes to hate.'

He turned to the crowd and jumped up on the bench again.

'They're giving you what you want now, but you can't trust them. I know you know that deep down. That feeling of unease. I know it's there in you. Hang on to that. You don't have to live under the rule of the Daleks. There's a resistance movement, you know. People among you who are brave enough to fight against the Daleks. Who know the secrets of what the Daleks are really doing here. I have met these people. I saw some of them killed, but there will be others. You should seek them out.'

The Doctor scanned across the eyes of the crowd. They were almost completely quiet again now. And he could sense that they were starting to listen.

'Seek who out?' asked the Dalek Litigator pointedly.

Then the Doctor heard the sound of shoes clicking on metal. He corkscrewed round immediately to look at the Dalek saucer. Five human figures were walking down the ramp from the hatchway. They were wearing dark coats with their hoods up. They had dark trousers and wore dark glasses. Three of them were women.

'Doctor…?' Lillian started to ask, sounding worried.

'What is this?' murmured the Doctor, uncertain.

As the figures reached the bottom of the ramp, they stopped a good few metres away from the Doctor. But they were close enough for him to see… To be sure that they were the resistance people he had seen murdered earlier today.

'Are these the resistance you talk of?' asked the Litigator.

'But… they were… Daleks exterminated them!' said the Doctor, making sure the crowd heard.

'He's right! They did!' shouted Sabel.

'Yeah, we were there!' chimed in Ollus.

'Evidence from the children is inadmissible,' said the Litigator.

'Inadmissible? What's the matter with you?' said the Doctor, jumping down to face the Litigator again. 'This isn't a court! I'm not on trial here!'

'You are now,' said the Litigator, swivelling to focus on the crowd. It continued to speak, now in loud, measured tones. 'The people who have just left my ship are care workers. They help people with paranoid delusions. They seek them out and care for them.'

'What, by lying to them?' scoffed the Doctor.

'By humouring them. By... *sympathising*,' the word sounded awkward for the Dalek to say.

'Oh, now I've heard it all!' said the Doctor, throwing his hands up in the air. 'So, I *imagined* the fact that Daleks killed these... people, is that it?'

'They are clearly alive,' said the Litigator.

'Except they're not, are they? Hmm?' said the Doctor. 'They're... What are they? Robomen? Duplicates? Reanimated dead filled with Dalek nanogenes? Take your pick!' He turned to the crowd again. 'The Daleks have an infinite number of tricks up their sleeves. They just love to control other people's minds. Makes it easier to get them to carry out their orders.'

'But...' said Lillian, clearly more confused than ever now. 'You said they were dead, Doctor.'

'They were. Are. They were never alive.' The Doctor could see that Lillian was wavering now.

'Lillian was one such patient who needed treatment,' said the Dalek Litigator. It slowly extended its suction arm to its full length, leaving the black cup at the end just a few centimetres short of Lillian.

The Doctor looked on in horror and disbelief.

'They contacted you to help you, Lillian,' said the Litigator in a soft, staccato tone.

'I... But...' she said, hesitating. A tear forming in one eye.

'Do you still trust the Doctor?' asked the Litigator. 'Are you sure he is telling the truth?'

'Lillian, you can't believe what this Dalek—' the Doctor started.

'I don't know. I'm not sure,' said Lillian. She was starting to break down. She clutched the children to her for support.

'Wait a minute, wait a minute,' said the Doctor, moving to Lillian, but the Litigator moved its suction arm to bar his way. The Doctor stumbled back, scanned across to the other Daleks, saw their gunsticks twitch in his direction.

'Do not try to influence her,' said the Litigator coolly. 'As you influence… the children.'

A rumble of disapproval was growing in the crowd.

'You told them their parents died because of the Daleks,' continued the Litigator. 'But what proof did you offer them? They only have your word for that.'

The Doctor could see that Sabel and Ollus were thinking about this. They were starting to look at the Doctor with uncertainty in their eyes… almost as if he were a stranger to them.

'Bring these… these "care workers" forward,' the Doctor said. 'Come on, let's see what they're really made of. Let everyone here see their faces. There's something not right about their faces.'

'They wear disguises,' said the Litigator.

'You see,' said the Doctor, pointing frantically, feeling he had won a point.

'To protect their anonymity for the sake of their patients,' continued the Litigator.

The Doctor could feel the crowd turn against him. In that moment, he knew he had lost them for good. What was worse, he could see Lillian no longer trusted him. A lifetime of unsettled feelings, of her true instincts

217

constantly telling her the whole Sunlight World set-up was a lie had taken its toll. He understood. With her mind filled with Dalek memory cells, how could she be sure of anything any more?

'I'm sorry,' he said to Lillian softly. 'I understand.'

Lillian could not speak. She merely shook her head slowly, tears now flowing. She seemed unable to look the Doctor directly in the eye.

He looked down at the children. They stepped back from him, confused, starting to be afraid.

The Doctor let out a long sigh. He nodded slowly at the Litigator.

'Gotta hand it to you,' he said, almost friendly in his tone. 'Never thought I'd see all this from a Dalek. Always got a surprise for me, haven't you?'

He looked back at the children. He looked into their eyes.

'You... you didn't go back for Jenibeth,' said Ollus accusingly, tears in his eyes.

'Oh,' said the Doctor. 'Like that, is it?' Then he crouched by them, looking at them on their level. They moved away from him again. He smiled. But they did not smile back. 'You don't want to go back to that orphanage, do you?' he asked them.

'It is the decision of this court...' started the Litigator.

'Oh... what are you up to now?' interrupted the Doctor.

'That these children should remain on Sunlight 349 in the custody of Lillian Belle,' said the Litigator.

Lillian held on to the children protectively.

'Oh, neat,' said the Doctor quietly. 'But what about

their sister, Jenibeth?'

There was a pause. The Litigator seemed to consider. For a moment, the Doctor thought he had gained some ground, that he had outwitted the Litigator. But he soon realised he was wrong.

'If the girl has been taken into protective custody by the Daleks—' it began.

'Protective custody!' the Doctor said mockingly. 'You have got to be kidding.'

'Then we will make all efforts to retrieve her and set her free,' said the Litigator.

Someone in the crowd shouted out 'Here, here!', provoking other cries of support for the Dalek Litigator. Slowly, applause started to break out. An applause that grew and grew until it roared with cheers.

The Doctor faced the Dalek Litigator. Its blank, ice-cold blue stare met him, unflinchingly. The Doctor felt sure that if it could have given a self-satisfied smile, it would have done. It had completely outmanoeuvred him. Only one question remained.

As the applause slowly died down, the Doctor seated himself on the bench nearby, folded his arms, kicked out his feet and said, 'So, what are you going to do with me?'

The crowd became hushed again.

'You won't hurt him, will you?' Sabel suddenly blurted out.

There was no reply, until…

A tiny, whining noise from above. The Doctor heard it first and looked up. Something blue and square was descending towards him. As it got lower in the sky, he could see he was staring at the bottom of the TARDIS, with the blue glow of Dalek thrusters at each corner. Four Daleks, their suckers firmly attached to the old police box shell, were carrying the TARDIS.

As they landed, the Daleks released their suction grip and the TARDIS thudded to the pavement.

'You're going to let me go?' asked the Doctor, in total disbelief. 'You're really letting me go?'

The Litigator withdrew its suction arm, then indicated the TARDIS with it.

'What are you up to?' asked the Doctor, gripped with suspicion.

All right, he thought, he would test this offer. He walked boldly to the TARDIS doors, put his hand in his pocket to find his key. He found it, but his hand also brushed against something else. Something smooth, small and cube-shaped. It was the message cube he had received from himself. It was still in his pocket, and it had re-formed.

Only pausing for a moment to think about this, the Doctor produced the TARDIS key and unlocked the doors. They swung open, creaking reassuringly. From inside, he could see the warm, orange-ish glow of the control room, the familiar sounds of his beloved ship drifting to his ears.

He looked around at the Dalek Litigator and the other Daleks. None of them was making a move to stop him.

'All right, then,' he said, still not sure what might happen next. 'Bye.'

He entered the TARDIS, then quickly stepped back

out. 'Since you're so touchy-feely and full of compassion for the children,' he said to the Dalek, his words dripping with sarcasm, 'Any objections to me saying goodbye to them?' He flicked a look at the crowd, then looked back at the Litigator. 'Since your faithful generation of Dalek citizens are watching?'

'Proceed,' said the Litigator in a low, flat tone.

The Doctor immediately marched up to the children. They looked up at him. Children who did not know what to think or feel now. The clever coercion of the Dalek Litigator had traumatised them even more, and the Doctor was certain of one thing. He would not make them feel worse. They had suffered enough. He would not plead for their understanding or try to change their minds. He would do just one thing. Something that he realised now was probably the most important thing of all.

He knelt down and took Ollus's hand. The little boy tried to pull it away.

'It's OK,' the Doctor said closely, in such a warm voice that Ollus relented for a moment. With the slightest sleight of hand, the Doctor had given the small white cube to Ollus. The little boy's eyebrows raised questioningly. The Doctor slowly shook his head and winked.

'If you ever think you need me,' whispered the Doctor, 'just hold this box and think of me. That's all.'

'Enough,' said the Litigator. 'You are upsetting the child.'

There were some boos from the crowd. But Sabel, Ollus and Lillian did not join in. They looked at the

Doctor, their faces showing they were confused. The Doctor simply smiled at them, rising to his feet, noticing that Ollus was slipping the cube into his pocket. With his other hand, the boy was holding his little spaceship.

'Aha,' the Doctor murmured to himself. He could feel ideas falling into place. He now knew what to do next.

The Doctor spun round, giving a big wave to everyone. He walked straight up to the Dalek Litigator and pointed directly into its blue eye lens.

'You think you're so clever, don't you?' said the Doctor. He dashed to the TARDIS and went inside, closing the door straight away. Then the door opened again. The Doctor poked his head out.

'But what if I'm cleverer?'

The door banged shut and, seconds later, the TARDIS dematerialised.

Chapter Fourteen
Call the Doctor

Nearly nine decades after the departure of the Doctor from Sunlight 349...

Ollus sat down in his favourite chair and looked out of the window of his comfy little room. The sun was shining as warmly as ever. He smiled as he saw his beloved little spaceship toy on the windowsill. It reminded him of his mother and father, though he barely remembered what they looked like now. Most of his memories had been kindly donated to him by his elder sister, Sabel, who lived in one of the other comfy rooms in the City Zone 004 Care Home for the Elderly.

He hadn't seen Sabel for a few days now. She'd had a cold and the nurses had told him it was best for her to be left alone to recover. He was missing her, but he understood that it was for the best.

Just then, there was a gentle knock at the door. Gill, his care attendant entered, smiling.

'Morning, Mr Blakely,' she said, in a sing-song sort of way. 'Did you enjoy your breakfast this morning?'

'Oh, I expect so,' Ollus said, smiling back at her. He spotted a tray with an empty plate, bowl and cup on it. Oh yes, he thought. He had enjoyed it. He remembered that now.

'And what shall we do today?' asked Gill. 'A little walk?'

'Oh yes, that would be nice,' he said, gaining the faint impression that this was what he did most days. 'How is Sabel?'

'Still a bit poorly, but the doctors say she'll be better in a day or two,' said Gill, mopping up some spilt juice then picking up the tray and heading for the door.

'The doctors,' said Ollus, suddenly deep in thought. He heard Gill stop at the door. She came padding back over to him.

'What is it, Mr Blakely?' she asked him.

'I knew a doctor once, you know,' he said. Suddenly, he could picture the Doctor, in his tweed jacket and bow tie, smiling at him, handing him something. He could feel the smooth sides of a small cube in his hand, almost as if he were actually touching it now.

'A doctor? Really?' asked Gill, perching on the side of Ollus's bed, next to his chair. 'Which doctor was this?'

'Oh, I'm not sure,' said Ollus, wrinkling up his old face as he tried to concentrate. 'So difficult to remember things these days, I'm afraid.' He squeezed his hand tight in his cardigan pocket as he tried to remember. Then he suddenly realised he actually had the small cube in his hand… now. Of course, yes. He remembered. He always kept this in his pocket. He brought it out and showed it to Gill.

Gill looked at the cube, fascinated.

'What's that?' she asked.

'I don't know,' said Ollus. 'The Doctor gave it to me. I remember that. He gave it to me... And he said...'

Ollus trailed off. He shut his eyes and started to feel a little uneasy. Was this a bad memory? Then, in his mind, through a warm haze, he saw the Doctor's face, smiling and winking. Perhaps it wasn't such a bad memory after all. Was it his? Or was it something Sabel had told him? He couldn't tell. Then he remembered the Doctor's words.

'He said, "If you ever think you need me, just hold this box and think of me." Yes, I remember that now. Nice, isn't it?' said Ollus, holding the little white cube up to the light. 'Nice thing to say. I think...'

And then he felt very tired. His arm started to waver.

'Oh, now then,' he heard Gill say, as his eyes started to close. 'You're tiring yourself out with all this remembering.'

He felt her hands help him to lie back as the chair reclined.

She probably put the cube back in my pocket, he thought as he drifted into sleep.

Probably.

Chapter Fifteen
Return to Gethria

Taking meticulous care not to cross his own timeline, the Doctor set the coordinates for the TARDIS to return to Gethria. He would arrive just moments after he had left that lonely little funeral near the great Cradle of the Gods monument.

His mind was now afire with a burning purpose. The Dalek Litigator may have outwitted him, but now he had an idea he knew how to defeat the entire Dalek plan.

The TARDIS engines thudded to a halt and the Doctor dashed down the steps of the control room and out onto the planet's surface. He had landed in exactly the same position as before. In the distance ahead of him, he could see the still, silent monument, now deserted, the mourners having left just a few minutes earlier.

He quickened his pace, breaking out into a slight sweat in the hot noon sun. As he neared the monument, he could see the gravestone, and there, embedded in it, along with other strange little items, was Ollus's precious spaceship toy. Just as it was when the Doctor had seen it for the very first time – a little old and worn, but definitely the same toy.

Reaching out to it, he stopped for a moment, feeling sad all of a sudden. This must have been Ollus's funeral. So who sent the message in the cube? Was it Ollus, when he knew he was close to the end of his life?

Blinking back the beginning of a tear, the Doctor firmly gripped the model spaceship in the stone. He pulled. It would not budge. This was going to need a bit of sonic technology to dislodge it.

Just as he was producing his sonic screwdriver to vibrate the little toy free, he was aware of a noise, over by the monument. A soft, shifting of sand.

He looked over, and there he saw an old woman standing by the great stone structure, dwarfed by its imposing scale. He looked hard at her. She was looking right back at him.

Slowly, she began to approach. As she got closer, he began to recognise her features. It was the old woman he had seen here before, when he had first observed the funeral in progress. She had stopped and looked at him, and then left.

Now she was back.

Then it suddenly struck him, as something in her eyes triggered another memory... This was one of the Blakely children.

'Is it...?' he started to ask as she arrived in front of him, smiling a somewhat haunted smile.

'Sabel,' she said in a brittle, old voice. 'Hello, Doctor.'

'Sabel?' said the Doctor. 'I came straight here.

Straight from saying goodbye to you and Ollus.'

He looked down at the gravestone.

'It's been a lifetime for us,' said Sabel. 'More than a lifetime.'

The Doctor nodded. Time travel did this kind of thing to him all the time. That was the nature of it. A twisty-turning thing that would tangle your hearts in barbs if you let it. He sniffed a thought-clearing sniff and reached out to touch Sabel's hand.

She withdrew it.

'Still not forgiven me, eh?' he said, nodding.

'*I* sent the message in the cube,' she said coldly. 'Ollus was too ill. He wanted to see you again, but…'

'I was too late…' said the Doctor, deeply saddened.

'Like you were too late to save our parents. Too late to save… Jenibeth,' said Sabel.

The Doctor felt those barbs in his hearts. He narrowed his gaze at Sabel. That was a cruel thing for her to say, but perhaps understandable. She had very possibly spent her life resenting the madman in a box who promised everything but delivered nothing.

He nodded. 'Understood,' he said. 'Now, if you'll excuse me, I have some business to attend to.'

He pointed his sonic screwdriver at the spaceship embedded in the stone. Activating it, he watched as it buzzed and the cement around the hull of the toy vibrated and crumbled.

'I know I can never make things better for you,' said the Doctor. 'But I can at least stop the Daleks.'

'Stop the Daleks?' there was an eagerness in her voice. Perhaps she would understand after all.

'Yes, this toy of Ollus's,' said the Doctor. 'I think this is what contains the activation codes for the Cradle of the Gods. I think Alyst and Terrin Blakely, your parents, couldn't resist making a record of their codes. Diligent physicists, you see. Catalogue and record everything. That's why this place came alive before, when Ollus was holding it.'

Then he stopped. It didn't quite make sense.

Thinking aloud, he said, 'Then why isn't it working now? Perhaps it's to do with proximity, and we were right inside that thing. Or... Hmm.' He would attempt to explain this to himself later, he decided. He switched off the sonic screwdriver.

'What are you going to do with it now?' asked Sabel.

'Destroy it,' he said. 'Smash it to pieces.'

Aware that Sabel was watching him intently, he put his hand on the little spaceship and started to pull it free of the gravestone.

Suddenly, Sabel's hand shot out and grabbed his. The shock he felt was not just caused by the suddenness, but by the sheer strength of her grip and...

The cold.

The icy cold touch of Sabel's hand. Colder than any *living* hand he had ever touched. Straining and failing to pull free of her iron grip, the Doctor looked Sabel straight in the eyes. She looked back at him with an emptiness that reminded him of the blankness of a Dalek's stare.

And then it happened...

A blue glow started to emerge through Sabel's forehead. A strange, unnerving, buzzing, cracking sound was rising. Her eyes remained fixed on him as a Dalek eyestalk burst through her bloodless skin, staring at him with its penetrating blue light.

Chapter Sixteen
A Billion Skaros

'Oh, Sabel,' the Doctor breathed. 'They got you, didn't they? The Daleks got you.'

In this moment of horror, the Doctor involuntarily relaxed his grip on the toy. With precise, mechanical reflexes, Sabel thrust the Doctor's hand aside and caught the little spaceship before it hit the ground.

The Doctor immediately made to grab the spaceship back but, with remarkable agility, she sidestepped him, then held up her other hand. The bloodless skin peeled back and the silver metal of a Dalek gun protruded unpleasantly from the flat of her palm.

'Do not move!' she intoned, harshly her old voice rasping, almost exactly like a Dalek's.

'They gave you Dalek nanogenes, didn't they?' murmured the Doctor, lamenting. 'Oh, Sabel...'

Suddenly, the air was filled with a thunderous burst of energy. A low, vibrating hum filled the Doctor's ears. He looked up. There, just to one side of the monument, a Dalek saucer was landing, having swooped down low at breathtaking speed.

The Doctor waited, accepting the inevitable, as the saucer's hatchway opened and the ramp slid down. Immediately, a squad of six Daleks moved rapidly down the ramp onto the sand, followed by one further Dalek, accompanied by two human figures. An old woman and an old man.

As the Dalek got closer and closer, the Doctor once again saw the quickly fading, blurring image on its grating. This was the Dalek Litigator again, returning to the scene of the crime. But more importantly for the Doctor, he suddenly knew that he could recognise the two elderly people being forced to keep pace with the Dalek.

Old and worn though their features were, they were unmistakably Ollus and…

Sabel?

He looked to the 'other' Sabel and back again to the new arrival. He found that this new Sabel was looking at the other, Dalek-converted woman. The Doctor realised that these women's faces were quite different. But there was a family resemblance.

'It's… Jenibeth,' said the newly arrived Sabel, a single tear furrowing down the lines of her noble old face.

Jenibeth? The Doctor realised that the Dalek-converted woman who had been threatening him was not Sabel at all, but her sister. The girl who had been taken prisoner by the Daleks decades ago.

'Jenibeth? It really… is you?' said Ollus, his tiny old voice cracking with emotion and disbelief.

'The Daleks sent the message in the cube to you,' the

Litigator stated, moving close to the Doctor.

'You?' the Doctor was dumbfounded.

'It contained a time-space tracer signal,' continued the Litigator, 'which proved most useful.'

'Then it was you, the Daleks,' started the Doctor, the terrible realisation dawning on him. 'You were the ones manipulating me. You've been following my every move.' He winced in annoyance at himself. 'Why am I even surprised?' He hit himself squarely on the forehead with the heel of his palm.

'They faked my funeral,' said Ollus. 'How impolite of them.'

'Well, I'm glad to see you're still alive, Ollus,' said the Doctor. 'And you, Sabel.'

'Only just,' the old man smiled. 'I'm afraid things get a bit confusing the older you get.'

'Tell me about it,' the Doctor said warmly.

'And I let my guard down,' continued Ollus. 'Just once. But once was enough. They got hold of the cube... somehow. I'm so sorry.'

'That's all right, Ollus, old chap,' shrugged the Doctor. 'Strictly speaking, it's a space-time anomaly. It shouldn't really exist, you know. Chicken and egg, egg and chicken, that sort of thing.' The Doctor was rambling now.

'Er... um, yes, well...' said Ollus, a little confused. 'But I didn't tell them anything about the spaceship.'

Sabel grabbed Ollus's arm in alarm. 'Ssh,' she said, suddenly realising her futility.

'Don't worry, Sabel,' said the Doctor, cross with himself. 'I think *I* just managed to give that little piece of information away before you arrived.'

'You will activate it!' commanded the Litigator. 'Activate the spaceship toy!'

'Oh, I don't think so,' replied the Doctor. 'You do your own dirty work.'

The Doctor was aware of the whine of Dalek traction coming from all around. The squad of other Daleks was converging upon them, swiftly ploughing through the sand towards them.

'You will activate the device or Ollus and Sabel will be exterminated!' commanded the Litigator.

Physically sagging with defeat, the Doctor sighed and put out his hand to Jenibeth. 'All right, then. Give it to me,' he said. 'I'm not sure exactly how it works, but I'll certainly give it my best shot.'

But before he could take the ship from Jenibeth, Ollus cried out, 'No!'

The Doctor stopped and looked at Ollus.

'We are old. We have lived our long lives,' said Ollus. Sabel encircled one of his arms with hers and held her brother close. She nodded, looking tearful but resolute. Ollus nodded back at her. 'Whatever this Cradle thing does, we can't let the Daleks have it, and that is surely worth our lives.'

The Doctor took hold of the tiny spaceship and looked into it. 'I won't balance lives, Ollus. I won't make noble gestures on behalf of others. It's not for me to sit in judgement.'

'But if the Daleks have this thing, they will have control of a terrible weapon!' pleaded Sabel.

'So what?' the Doctor suddenly proclaimed, full of

bluster and a trifle petulantly. 'The Daleks are always getting awesome weapons and threatening to blow things up or whatever their latest, overblown plan is. I'll find a way to defeat them. It's what I do. It's inevitable. I always defeat them… mostly.' Then he turned to the Dalek Litigator, dismissively. 'How bad can this Cradle actually be anyway?'

'It will *transform* the Sunlight Worlds,' said the Litigator.

'Transform them?' the Doctor was worried now. 'Transform? How?'

'They will be turned into a billion Skaros,' said the Litigator.

'A billion…? How can you make a billion versions of your home planet?' demanded the Doctor. He looked hard at the Dalek Litigator, but it remained silent.

'Come on, out with it!' said the Doctor. 'I'm at your mercy, aren't I? Or are you still scared of me?'

At that moment, the Doctor doubled up in pain. Something powerful was lancing right through his mind. He gasped and strained through the agony to look up.

There. He saw it again. The whirling blur in the middle of the Litigator's grating. But this time it was larger, more defined and swirling with a glowing power that filled his mind with the sickening feeling of falling headlong into an abyss. He suddenly realised he was looking directly into the Time Vortex. Here, on this Dalek's casing, the Time Vortex seemed to be pulling the Doctor in…

Snapping back upright, the Doctor tried to pull

himself together. He stared back at the Dalek Litigator again and, to his horror, he realised it had transformed into something else. Another Dalek, but a Dalek whose casing seemed to shift constantly in colour and shape. Across the grating, rotating rings, like compressed versions of those of a gas giant planet spun unfathomably.

'The Dalek Time Controller,' the Doctor said, the words almost choking in his throat. 'I should have known.'

'You – know – me?' the Dalek Time Controller asked, with a far less mechanical voice than any other Dalek known to the Doctor.

'Oh yes,' said the Doctor. 'But don't expect me to tell you how or why. That'll be for you to find out, one day. Sorry, secrets of a Time Lord, I'm afraid. So, you were behind all this. Of course you were.'

'Now, you will activate the toy,' instructed the Time Controller.

'The funny thing is,' said the Doctor, starting to chuckle to himself, 'I don't actually know how it works. When we were here before, it must have just sort of started doing stuff. We didn't do anything clever, did we, Ollus?'

Without warning, Ollus leapt forward towards the Doctor and snatched the toy from him. He raised his hand high in the air as if to smash the little spaceship down, then froze, as if all his nerves and muscles had locked into place.

'No, Ollus!' the Doctor called out. 'You idiot! You've touched it!'

All at once, a deep rumbling sound erupted from behind them all. The Doctor, the Time Controller and everyone else turned to the Cradle of the Gods. The giant stones were shifting. Shafts of light were bursting forth from it. Energy was fizzing all over the structure. The power was growing and growing as every minute passed.

'It wasn't just the toy,' said the Doctor to Ollus and Sabel. 'I felt it… when this happened before. It gets into your mind. The toy is just the conduit. The technology of the Cradle is activated through your minds, through all the fragments of your parents' research hiding in there, in long-forgotten memories. The actual codes your father recorded and put in the toy's simple little memory form the key that unlocks those fragments. Mental power is what the Cradle feeds on!'

Ollus winced, cried out and then collapsed, still holding the toy. He started to sob. Sabel was putting a hand to her head, clearly experiencing some pain too.

'It's affecting both of you,' said the Doctor, kneeling to comfort Ollus. The Doctor threw a glance at Jenibeth, who had been standing stock still throughout, as if her mind had been switched off. For a moment, he thought he saw her face twitch.

Then another crash from the Cradle drew the Doctor's attention away. The stones had moved and locked into an entirely new formation. At the front of the monument, facing them, was a large alcove, covered in glowing symbols.

'Hogoosta's research gave us the way of programming the Cradle,' announced the Time

Controller, triumphantly. It began to glide towards the control alcove. 'All we needed was the activation code.'

'So what are you going to do?' shouted the Doctor at the Controller's back. He was now steadying poor Sabel, who had fallen to her knees, sobbing.

'Once programmed, the Cradle will transmit an energy wave across the Sunlight Worlds, converting the raw atomic material we invested in those planets into a billion Skaros, teeming with Dalek life!'

The Time Controller reached the alcove, clamping its suction cup in sequence to the many and varied control indentations. Immediately, the Cradle started to react, with deep rumbles of power shuddering through it.

'Atomic material,' muttered the Doctor in disgust. 'That's all those people and their ideal Sunlight Worlds were for you, weren't they? Just a collection of matter, some of it intelligent and organic, to be reprogrammed by this... this obscenity!'

The Dalek Time Controller continued making its adjustments, ignoring the Doctor now.

'I remember.'

The Doctor, Sabel and Ollus turned. It was the voice of Jenibeth.

'I remember being here before,' she muttered, a tear falling down her face. She turned to face the others. 'Sabel! Ollus!' she uttered, in sheer joy.

'She remembers?' asked Ollus. 'Is that possible, after what the Daleks have done to her?'

The Doctor glanced from Jenibeth to the Cradle and back again. 'Yes,' he proclaimed, a broad smile growing across his face. 'Yes! It's the energy from the Cradle. It's getting into her mind. A mind preserved by the Dalek nanogenes. A strong, young mind.'

'I remember... everything sparkled here,' said Jenibeth. 'Then you all left me. I was all alone for so long. So very long.'

Sabel struggled to her feet and ran to her sister, embracing her. 'Oh, Jenibeth, how did you survive all this time?'

'You told me to think of jelly blobs,' said Jenibeth simply, starting to smile. 'That's what I did. All the time. I think... think of them all the time.'

Despite sounding like an old woman, her voice and manner had a childlike quality, the Doctor realised. Imprisoned by the Daleks for a whole lifetime, she had had no education, no adult life. All she had had to sustain her were childish thoughts of her favourite thing. Jelly blobs.

Sabel gripped her sister even tighter, looking over her shoulder at the Doctor, her tears still flowing. Another personal tragedy caused by the Daleks, the Doctor thought. They never stopped causing tragedies of any and every magnitude. It was their speciality and he hated them for it. Hated them like he knew he could never hate anything else.

'What have you done?' came the sudden, accusing, shrill tones of the Dalek Time Controller.

The Doctor turned round to see the Time Controller disengaging from the Cradle's controls.

'Oh dear,' laughed the Doctor. 'Having a bit of trouble, are we?'

'Come here or I will exterminate you!' commanded

the Dalek, its voice wracked with frustration.

'Don't help them,' gasped Ollus, struggling to stand up as the Doctor walked slowly across the sand to the monument.

'I won't,' whispered the Doctor as he passed Ollus, winking.

The Doctor walked right into the control alcove.

'May I?' he asked the Dalek Time Controller. The Dalek moved out of his way so that the Doctor could get to the controls. Taking a deep breath, he put both his hands on a couple of the glowing symbols.

Immediately, the Doctor felt the same, intrusive sensation in his mind that he had felt that last time he had been on Gethria, when the Cradle had started to activate then. Something was burrowing into his thoughts. But this time it was different, he was starting to see something, a thought solidifying into a solid image.

Then he started to laugh.

'What is it?' asked the Time Controller, clearly irritated. 'Do not make that disagreeable noise!'

'I'm sorry,' gasped the Doctor, containing his laughter. 'I just saw something in my head. Something this gigantic piece of planet-creating technology is singularly concentrating on. Something big and colourful and... juicy!'

'I do not understand!' said the Controller, its eye lens shining brighter than ever, the lights on its dome burning with rage.

'This technology has fixed onto the strongest mind here containing fragments of its activation code,' said the Doctor, leaning close to the Dalek, spitting the words at it through gritted teeth. 'Jenibeth's. The mind you left in a childlike state for a whole lifetime. A mind you tortured through solitude and imprisonment. A poor young girl whose only escape from her endless incarceration was her one childish pleasure. Jelly blobs!'

'Jelly...?' the Dalek Time Controller swivelled its dome uncomprehendingly.

'Sweets! Big jelly blob sweets!' shouted the Doctor. 'This great, planet-creating bit of ancient machinery is about to take all your carefully prepared atomic material on the Sunlight Worlds and turn it into a load of planet-sized jelly blobs! Not quite your plan, eh? Extreme Confectionary Death of the Daleks!'

'Alter the programming immediately!' the Dalek demanded.

'No!' said the Doctor. 'Why should I? Anyway, I don't know how. Oh...'

And then he suddenly realised...

'A billion Skaros may have just been avoided, but the conversion of the Sunlight Worlds into giant jelly blobs is still going to wipe out countless billions of lives. Oh dear.'

'So be it!' Clearly the Time Controller had reached the same conclusion. 'The Sunlight Worlds will be destroyed. The human empire's economy and social fabric will collapse. Humanity will suffer!'

'Oh, listen to yourself,' the Doctor said in disgust. 'Glorying in the suffering of others. You sicken me.'

'Thus weakened,' concluded the Dalek, 'the human race will easily be conquered by the Daleks!'

'Pretty happy with Plan B, then, are we?' said the Doctor. 'Well, *I'm not!*'

Straight away, the Doctor started working on the Cradle's controls as the hum of its power started to rise in pitch and grow in intensity. It wasn't going to be long now before the Cradle sent forth its deadly wave of matter-converting energy.

'What are you doing?' demanded the Time Controller.

'Er... nothing,' lied the Doctor, as he quickly operated the controls in the most illogical sequence he could think of. Suddenly, the image of jelly blobs in his mind changed to a raging, chaotic maelstrom of exploding energy. 'Ah,' concluded the Doctor. 'Actually, I think I may have just set it to self-destruct.'

Immediately, the Dalek Time Controller aimed its weapon at the Doctor. Seeing this, the Doctor cringed helplessly and closed his eyes.

There was the searing, blasting sound of the Dalek gun firing.

Then...

Nothing.

The Doctor opened his eyes, surprised that he was still alive. The Dalek Time Controller was moving rapidly away. The Doctor looked around, bamboozled about what had actually happened.

Then he saw Jenibeth, standing close by, her hand outstretched, the Dalek gun protruding from it. She fired again and made a direct hit. A fizz of garish blue, sizzling energy engulfed the Time Controller. It clearly had extra force-field shielding, or maybe it was its connection with the Time Vortex that was protecting it. The Doctor had no idea, but he could see that the Time Controller was anything but keen about being shot again.

'Under attack!' it was screeching. 'Exterminate! Exterminate them all!'

The other Daleks started to open fire.

With remarkable agility, Jenibeth leapt up into the air, tumbling, firing repeatedly. Her beams lanced expertly into four of the six attacking Daleks, cutting open their casings and frying the mutant creatures inside.

The Doctor heard their shrieking death throes as he frantically recommenced his work on the ancient Cradle technology. The trouble was, he had just *stumbled* upon a way to make it blow up – he was good at making things blow up, he had had a lot of experience. But now, he had no idea what he was doing.

'Get down, Sabel! Ollus!' Jenibeth was crying out as she opened fire again.

The remaining two Daleks and the Dalek Time Controller immediately elevated, flying up into the air to gain tactical advantage, firing down at Jenibeth. An impact explosion behind her knocked her flat to the ground. She crawled for cover behind a rock, firing up and destroying her attacker with one blast.

'Leave them!' commanded the Dalek Time Controller, heading for the Dalek saucer. 'Leave them all to die!'

The surviving Dalek drone obeyed immediately and headed straight into the saucer. Following it, the Dalek Time Controller swivelled its mid-section and fired back one shot before it disappeared into its spacecraft. The beam was still lancing towards its target as the saucer's power activated and the great ship started to lift off.

The beam bounced into the structure of the monument and then deflected downwards, hitting Jenibeth full in the chest.

Jenibeth could see the sky.

She was cold.

Then faces moved in front of the sky. Three faces. One was a young man. The other two were old.

'There's only one chance,' the young man was saying. 'The Cradle may still be locked into Jenibeth's mind.'

He had said 'Jenibeth'. He must know her, she thought.

'It may still be taking its atomic matter conversion settings from her. If she concentrates hard enough, she may be able to override the self-destruct,' the man was saying.

'What are you thinking about, Jenibeth?' asked the old man.

'Can you hear us?' asked the old woman. 'I think she's gone, Doctor.' The old woman cried. Her tears fell down onto Jenibeth's face, splattering, wet.

'Jelly blobs,' Jenibeth felt herself say. Her voice sounded old and gravelly. Strange. 'I'm thinking of jelly blobs. Sabel told me to think of them.'

'We've got to get her to think about something else,' said the man the old lady had called 'Doctor'. 'I've got it!' he said, seeming to be very pleased indeed. But everything was getting quiet now. The sky seemed to be getting darker. She couldn't hear anything else the man was saying.

Then suddenly, just when she thought she would drift off to sleep, she heard a voice so close to her that she felt her eyes open with a start. Then another voice. A voice either side of her. Two old, kindly voices and they were saying such wonderful things.

They were telling her a story of worlds where the sun always shone, where the people were happy. Where you could live a whole life in contentment. They told her of their lives there and how happy and comfortable they had been.

They had, they said, only one sadness… That their mother, father and sister had been lost to them. And as she listened more and more to the lovely story the warm voices were telling her, she realised she was part of this story; that they were *her* parents that were lost and that *she* was the sister these voices had missed so much.

And just as everything seemed so cold and dark and that she would stop thinking altogether, she felt herself engulfed in such a warmth as she had never felt before. Yet, somehow, it felt right. It felt like the best kind of warmth and happiness there could ever be.

Suddenly, everything felt new.

The energy wave from the Cradle of the Gods was surging upwards into the sky; a broiling mass of impossible colours getting brighter, ever brighter. The Doctor shielded his eyes and looked down at Sabel and Ollus, both of them speaking softly but with great determination into Jenibeth's ears. But Jenibeth was still and silent, her eyes staring up, unblinking into the apocalyptic chaos.

'It's too late. I'm sorry,' the Doctor called to them. 'Come on, we have to take shelter in the TARDIS or the Cradle's energy will destroy us.'

But Sabel and Ollus gave no sign of having heard him.

The Doctor stumbled forwards, starting to feel as though his body was being crushed by a merciless increase in gravity.

'Run! Run back to the TARDIS,' he was saying. 'I'll carry Jenibeth, but you must—'

His words were cut off as great, corkscrewing shafts of burning energy suddenly slammed into the desert, seeming to rock the very foundations of Gethria. Like gigantic, writhing, gnarled tree roots impossibly fashioned from the fiery matter of stars, they seemed to surge ceaselessly both upwards and downwards at the same time. Each titanic impact created its own shockwave with a force like ten thousand hurricanes.

Squinting desperately through all this, the Doctor tried to blink the burning sand from his raw eyes, searching for Sabel, Ollus and Jenibeth. His mind was whirling with the effects of concussion as he realised he had been propelled a hundred metres or more by a shockwave. Picking himself up, every fibre of him fighting against the energy that was combusting in the air all around him now, he started to make his way back to the siblings.

They were now barely visible to him as he tried to struggle onwards. But although he was exerting all the energy of a full-powered sprint, he gradually became aware that he was barely moving at all. He called as loudly as he could, but he found his voice made no sound.

Gathering himself and applying every ounce of energy he could muster, the Doctor was suddenly hit by another shockwave.

Consciousness drained from his mind. All he could feel was the sensation of flying, tumbling... A dull, hard impact.

Then he was awake again.

Almost blind now, he reached out and felt the familiar, wooden shell of the TARDIS. Instinctively, he reached up, finding the key to the door was already in his hand. He unlocked the door, pushed it open, then attempted to look back.

Gethria was now an unrelenting mass of burning energy. But he would try again to find those Blakelys.

He could not leave them. He *would* not leave them.

Then another blast hit him, pushing him through the now open TARDIS doors.

He crashed to the floor of the TARDIS control room, barely aware that the doors had slammed shut behind him.

Of course they closed, he suddenly found himself thinking. You clever thing, you.

He patted the floor in an utterly exhausted gesture of affection, as the ship juddered violently. Explosions and smoke were everywhere, and the Doctor wondered for a moment if the TARDIS had finally met its match. Whether the Gethrian monument, sending its energy wave out to engulf Gethria and the Sunlight Worlds, had the ancient power to rip his old space-time machine apart...

In a way, the Doctor felt, it was perhaps no more than he deserved.

He tried to reassure himself that he had done his best. But in the final analysis, he had left Ollus and Sabel with their dying sister, Jenibeth.

The Doctor who kept meddling in the affairs of others, who lit the blue touch paper then ran for the hills. He had done it again.

Never again, he thought. Things were going to change. And soon.

He breathed a sigh of relief as the juddering ebbed away and the TARDIS steadied. He rubbed the sand painfully from his red eyes.

When he ventured outside, he feared the worst...

The sky was dazzling. The power the Cradle had released was apparently still present everywhere. The desert was awash with sizzling energy, sending clouds of dust into the sky. Through it all, the Doctor could make out the monument, still towering but no longer alight with its ancient, elemental forces.

Gripped by a grim determination to discover what had happened, the Doctor ran at full pelt towards the monument. His feet pounded through the sand. Energy crackled and burnt, splattering sparks and sand in his face; but he kept running. Running to the exact spot where he knew he had left Ollus, Sabel and Jenibeth.

He finally reached it.

The dust and flashes of dissolving power slowly cleared. He peered down, fearing... expecting the worst.

What he saw filled him with an overwhelming joy and wonder. Such was the force of it that it sent him crashing to his knees. He wiped tears from his eyes.

'Well, hello there,' he said.

He found himself looking at Ollus, Sabel and Jenibeth... But they were children, as he had known them when he had first met them.

'Well, this is...' he paused. 'Unexpected.'

He had told the old Ollus and Sabel to tell Jenibeth about the Sunlight Worlds. To describe them in every detail, to convince her how peaceful and worthwhile they were. The idea was to change the matter-creating wave of energy from the Cradle into a force that would either recreate or preserve the Sunlight Worlds as they were.

But somehow, Ollus and Sabel had gone further. Perhaps they had idealised their story of the Sunlight Worlds too much. They must have created a vision of their happiest times together...

When they were children.

The matter conversion wave had done the rest, taking as its template the thoughts from the mind it was locked into. The thoughts of Jenibeth Blakely.

Just as the Doctor was pondering what to do or say next, and whether or not these newly atomically reconstructed children would even know who he was, there was an enormous crashing sound.

Another spaceship had landed. An oddly familiar spaceship. It was, he realised, the craft that Alyst and Terrin Blakely had chartered to bring their family here, to Gethria.

The children turned to look at the spaceship, and the Doctor found himself slowly backing away. He could see that two people were exiting the craft.

As he backed away faster and faster, he stopped and lingered just long enough to see if what he suspected was true.

Yes, the two people were Alyst and Terrin Blakely, recreated from the mind of their daughter.

The Doctor turned and ran back to the TARDIS as fast as he could go. He closed the door behind him and rushed to the console, panting hoarsely. He switched on the scanner and adjusted it to view local space.

There, he could see the Sunlight Worlds, still intact. He made some adjustments and turned up the volume on the speaker. Slowly, he began to make out the sounds of life from these worlds. A cacophony of transmissions. He even fancied for a moment that he could make out the voice of Lillian Belle.

Satisfied, he set the TARDIS in motion. The old engines heaving back into life.

He shook his head, still in a daze of disbelief. He felt like he had just participated in some crazy dream. A dream that had been made real by the ancient powers of an unfathomably mysterious technology. A technology the Daleks had set out to harness and turn into a force for destruction. A technology which, the Doctor noted with a broad, beaming smile, had ended up doing exactly the opposite.

'Ha!' he found himself saying aloud. 'One in the eye for you, Daleks!'

But it had been a close run thing. Things could so easily have gone the other way. Billions could have died.

Feeling cold inside, he thought of all those he had

lost during his long life and resolved to learn his lesson once and for all.

'No more meddling,' he said. 'No more.'

As Ollus, Sabel and Jenibeth embraced their delighted but baffled parents, Sabel turned and looked across the desert, away from the huge monument before them.

'Did you see that man, Mummy?' she asked.

'What man?' asked Alyst Blakely.

'I didn't see a man,' said Ollus, pulling his tiny spaceship from his pocket.

'Neither did I,' said Jenibeth, tucking into another packet of jelly blobs.

'I think you must have imagined him,' said Terrin Blakely.

Sabel looked out across the desert. For a moment, she thought she had heard a strange, groaning noise. But no, there was nothing now.

BBC

DOCTOR WHO

Plague of the Cybermen

JUSTIN RICHARDS

'They like the shadows.'

'What like the shadows?'

'You know them as Plague Warriors…'

When the Doctor arrives in the 19th-century village of Klimtenburg, he discovers the residents suffering from some kind of plague – a 'wasting disease'. The victims face a horrible death – but what's worse, the dead seem to be leaving their graves. The Plague Warriors have returned…

The Doctor is confident he knows what's really happening; he understands where the dead go, and he's sure the Plague Warriors are just a myth.

But as some of the Doctor's oldest and most terrible enemies start to awaken, he realises that maybe – just maybe – he's misjudged the situation.

A thrilling, all-new adventure featuring the Doctor as played by Matt Smith in the spectacular hit series from BBC Television.

U.S. $9.99 (Canada: $11.99) ISBN: 978-0-385-34676-4

BBC

DOCTOR WHO

Shroud of Sorrow

TOMMY DONBAVAND

23 November 1963

It is the day after John F. Kennedy's assassination –
and the faces of the dead are everywhere. PC Reg
Cranfield sees his recently deceased father in the mists
along Totter's Lane. Reporter Mae Callon sees her late
grandmother in a coffee stain on her desk. FBI Special
Agent Warren Skeet finds his long-dead partner staring
back at him from raindrops on a window pane.

Then the faces begin to talk, and scream... and push
through into our world.

As the alien Shroud begins to feast on the grief of a
world in mourning, can the Doctor dig deep enough into
his own sorrow to save mankind?

*A thrilling, all-new adventure featuring the Doctor and Clara,
as played by Matt Smith and Jenna-Louise Coleman in the
spectacular hit series from BBC Television.*

U.S. $9.99 (Canada: $11.99) ISBN: 978-0-385-34678-8